Gorgeous George

And the Unidentified, Unsinkable Underpants

Part 02

By

Stuart Reid

Illustrations, Cover and Layouts
By John Pender

D1331937

i

Gorgeous Garage Publishing Ltd
Falkirk, Scotland

Cover design and illustrations by John Pender
Cover and illustrations copyright © Gorgeous Garage Publishing Ltd

Photographs used by kind permission
of Jess Reid and John Pender

Third Edition
This edition published in the UK by
Gorgeous Garage Publishing Ltd
ISBN 978-1-910614-07-5

www.stuart-reid.com

DEDICATION

To John, for fate and good fortune

To the Society of Authors and the Authors
Foundation for their support

To Audrey, for everything else

Oh yeah, and my girls. I have to mention
Jess and Charley again.
(They made me do it!)

Reading Rocks!

*For my wife Angela and my little boy Lucas.
Who's love, encouragement and unrelenting
patience means the absolute world me.*

*Thank you for letting daddy
live out his drawing dream!*

*Love always,
John xXx*

(And Stuart... you're very welcome!)

CONTENTS

Prologue

The earth shifted. Not much but enough.

No one noticed, at first. It wasn't an earthquake or even a tremor, just an underground rumbling like the giant belly of a hungry beast. Far below the surface rocks fell. Caverns and passageways that had lain open for millions of years were sealed at one critical junction. Tunnels and fissures in the earth's crust were opened and underground rivers were diverted.

Water stopped flowing down and started flowing out.

The Story So Far...

Grandpa Jock had stuffed two large whoopee cushions into his pants.

Actually, he hadn't just shoved them in, in any sort of haphazard fashion. He'd carefully sewn special pockets into his underwear that allowed the whoopee cushions to be slipped into the rear part of the pants for a bit of extra padding. You see, Grandpa Jock was bothered with piles.

Haemorrhoids, to be exact. Little itchy, scratchy nodules that sprout out of people's bottoms as they grow older, making it quite uncomfortable to sit down for long periods of time. And, if you're not too embarrassed, you need to go along to the doctor's, stick your bum in his face and let him inspect them. Then the doctor usually recommends an operation and more doctors and nurses need to prod around up your bottom.

Grandpa Jock didn't really fancy that. So he invented his special cushioned underpants, complete with blown up whoopee cushion padding, that didn't blast off when he sat down because he used extra strong duct tape to seal them shut.

Okay, his bum looked a little bit bigger underneath his kilt but he could sit down in comfort and that's all that mattered to the mad old Scotsman.

His grandson Gorgeous George (he's not really gorgeous but some older girls had teased him once and the nickname kinda stuck) and his friends Allison (sensible, responsible and way too mature for her age) and Crayon Kenny (ridiculously barking-mad boy with a habit of sticking crayons and any other small object in his ears, up his nose, in his belly button and anywhere else you care to think of (but don't think too hard. Yeah, up there too!)) have all joined Grandpa Jock on a camping trip to Loch Ness in Scotland.

Grandpa Jock is there to reclaim the crown of the World Porridge Making Championships after it was won last year by a bunch of mad Mexican bandits and their special Chilli Chocolate Porridge. He couldn't bear to see foreigners teaching the Scots how to make their second national dish. Of course, haggis will always be No.1!

After losing a fight with a tent but winning his battle with some tricky trouser trumpets, Grandpa Jock entered the porridge tournament only to discover that every porridge dish in the competition had been sabotaged; spiked with a range of vile ingredients from salt to mustard to dynamite and even rabbit poo. The tournament was postponed until the following day (Monday) when security was to be beefed up.

George, Kenny and Allison had met a little Highland lad called Hamish, who was smaller in height but slightly older than them. Hamish told them about a strange encounter he'd had with a large creature out on Loch Ness the previous week. This experience had been so freaky that Hamish's big brother Angus had immediately wet his pants and locked himself in his bedroom for a week. He still wasn't out yet.

And for some reason, George was being a miserable little git this weekend. He'd hoped this trip was going to be a lads' holiday but his mum had persuaded Allison's mum to send Allison along too, to keep an eye on things. George's mum didn't trust Grandpa Jock not to get into trouble.

Then George went in the huff because Allison had been promoted to Grandpa Jock's special helper, working in the kitchen, looking after all the food, the pots, the pans and even buying those extra special ingredients like garlic, raisins and stalks of asparagus (although George had never seen his grandpa making porridge with asparagus before) – and Allison had bought loads of it.

The fact that Allison had won a prize in one of the categories of the Porridge Poetry Competition had sent George into an ever fouler mood. He'd thought his poem about a little poo who jumped down the toilet, became leader of a poo army and tried to take over the world was a classic but it hadn't gone down too well with the judges.

And while all this was going on, a team of American super-geek scientists were trying to work out why there was a drought in England and all the lakes were drying up south of the border, whilst Loch Ness was overflowing with saltier, more acidic water; a phenomenon that had not been witnessed in over 10,000 years. Professor Marmaduke Spicer, or Marmy to his friends, was the leader of these scientists. He was a professor of palaeontology and cryptozoology, the biggest ever brain to walk out of Harvard University and a lover of all this porridgy.

Doctor Peewee Peterson was a geologist and hydrologist who'd spent his entire career studying puddles; which is probably why his three wives left him, although, er... not all at once, you understand – surprisingly, he'd found three different women to marry him at various times. Peewee was first to admit that he was the most boring scientist in the world. He had an IQ of 207 and listed his hobbies as 'looking at rocks'.

Commander Charles 'Chuck' Choppers was an aquamarine biologist, a former US Navy Oceanographer and a deep disappointment to his father, who was hoping for an all-American action hero for a son. So much so, that his dad forced him into military school as soon as he started calling his pet tadpoles girly names. At military school, Chuck learnt to shoot machine guns, play with explosives, drive tanks, sail submarines and even fly helicopters but he preferred reading books and studying for his exams. He was probably the skinniest, geekiest, highly trained, combat killing machine the world had ever seen.

So now George, Kenny, Allison, Hamish and Grandpa Jock find themselves out in the middle of Loch Ness on a little boat in the early hours of the morning on a mental monster hunt. No clue what they're doing, no life jackets and no common sense.

And there's something in the water?

Chapter 16 – In The Water (From Part 1)

'What's that?!' shouted Kenny, pointing off into the distance.

'What? Where?' yelled everybody else.

'That black shape looming up out of the water. Can't you see it?'

George peered ahead screwing his eyes up and focussing on the black water line. 'I see it too. There's something out there.' Hamish smiled.

'Oh my goodness, it's huge,' shrieked Allison, as her eyes began to make out the tall, dark mass in front of the boat. It was approaching slowly... slowly... slowly...

'Raaaarrrrrrrr!' growled Grandpa Jock.

'Aaaargh!' shrieked George, Allison and Kenny.

'What a fright, Grandpa!?' complained George. 'I nearly jumped out the boat then.'

'That'll teach you for laughing at me when I nearly pooped my pants,' giggled Grandpa Jock, pleased he'd gotten his own back so soon.

'What about the monster though?' Kenny was still pointing at the shape looming up in the blackness.

'That's Cherry Island, ya tube,' laughed Hamish. 'We're almost at the southern-most tip of the loch. Fort Augustus is down there.'

'You mean that's the island?' George didn't believe his eyes any more than Kenny did. The night was becoming darker now and murky shadows merged into each other.
BUMP!
The boat bounced a little.

'What was that?' screeched Kenny, who was normally calm but now, for some reason, was becoming more nervous by the minute.

'Be chilled, man,' hushed Hamish. 'We're probably

brushing over the remains of Dog Island. It's submerged around here somewhere.'

'Are you sure? I would've said that was more of a 'bump' than a 'brush'.' Kenny was holding onto the edge of the boat, staring frantically at the surface of the water.

'Take it easy, Kenny,' said George, trying to reassure his friend.

'Take it easy? Take it blooming easy, he says!' Kenny was breathing hard. 'We're out here hunting giant prehistoric monsters in a little wooden boat and you want me to take it easy.'

'We don't know if there's a Loch Ness monster. We haven't seen anything yet,' asked Allison.

'Well, I've changed my mind. I don't want to see anything. I should've stayed on dry land.'

'Don't worry. We'll need to stay dry anyway; I've forgotten to bring the life jackets with us.' Hamish shrugged.

'It's okay,' reassured Grandpa Jock. 'No one's going in the water.'

BUMP!

The boat rocked to and fro, violently this time. Hamish cut the motor.

'See! See, definitely more 'bump' than 'brush' that time.'

'Did you see that? Off the starboard bow?' asked Allison, turning across to the side of the boat.

'Now she decides to get all nautical on us!' Kenny was close to freaking out. 'What's the starboard side?'

Grandpa Jock had stood up and stepped over the centre board. He put his hand on Kenny's shoulder.

'That's the starboard bow there, to the front right of the boat. 'Port' is the left hand side. Now, what did you see, girl?'

'There! Again!' Allison had turned to see if Grandpa Jock was looking in the right place.

'Yes! I saw it too,' George had seen something. Yes, he wanted to agree with Allison, to make amends, to support her but he really had seen something and he pointed to the water between the boat and the island.

A large, black scaly hide slipped below the water's surface and disappeared.

'I told you. I told you!' Hamish kept repeating. Kenny slunk deeper into the bottom of the boat. Allison sat alongside him. His face was chalk white and he'd stopped looking out at the water. He'd seen enough.

Three black humps rose silently from the water and slipped away again, this time on the far side of the boat. A mass of bubbles broke through the surface and gurgled on the water, followed by soft pink bobbing up then quickly back below. Another shape swam passed the boat, closer this time and several shadows circled in the depths but it was too dark to make out their true form.

Something small and dark broke through the water.

'A fin!' shouted Allison, jumping up and pointing out the back of the boat. She was standing on the bench near the bow. Kenny sat upright, his head nudging against Allison's legs.

A dark, diamond-shaped flipper glided across the water for a few seconds then disappeared below into the blackness.

BUMP!

The boat rocked.

Allison toppled backwards and plunged in the water.

'Allison! No!' cried George, reaching out to catch her. Grandpa Jock jumped forward and threw out his hand. Hamish grabbed an oar.

For a second Allison was visible on the surface. Hamish tried using the hook end of the oar to catch at her clothes but she sank away into the gloom.

'ALLISON!' shouted George, pulling off his jumper, ready to dive in. Hamish hauled him back by his arm.

'Ye can't, George. One in the water is bad enough. There are strong currents below the surface that can drag any swimmer into the deep.'

'That's why I have to save her!'

'No, he's right, lad. You can't go in,' said Grandpa Jock. 'Help me search with this oar.' They scanned the water for any sign of life. Allison was nowhere to be seen.

Kenny and Hamish worked frantically with one oar, Grandpa Jock and George with the other, pulling the paddles through the water hoping to snag the hook on Allison's clothes or something, anything. The water was black and murky.

Instinctively George turned.

'There she is!' he screamed.

About ten metres behind the boat, George could see Allison's hand just breaking the surface, reaching upwards.

'Something's dragging her,' Grandpa Jock whispered.

'Come on, turn the boat Turn the boat!' George began thrashing at the water with his hands. Hamish and Grandpa dug the oars into the water and the boat slowly edged around.

'She's going under again,' shouted Kenny, pulling at the water with George.

Allison's hand slipped from view into the blackness.

In the few seconds that it took until the boat reached the spot, Allison had disappeared. There was no trace, no bubbles or not even a shadow below the water.

Grandpa Jock and Hamish plunged the oars as deep as they dared but the loch held onto its secrets.

Allison was gone.

End of Part 1

Gorgeous George and the
Unidentified Unsinkable Underpants Part 2

Chapter 17 – Drowning

Silence engulfed the small boat. The loch was still and the water was flat.

There was no moon but the sky was filled with an ocean of stars. They sparkled overhead and danced in the tiny ripples that lapped off the hull.

George sat in the well of the boat with his head in his hands. He sobbed quietly.

Kenny and Hamish were at the stern, sitting either side of the motor. They stared ahead, their eyes filled with tears, their minds filled with a shocking numbness of disbelief and anguish.

Grandpa Jock held onto the sides as he stared into the water. He'd been standing there, searching for thirty minutes. Allison had been under the water a long time.

'I'm sorry, lad,' he said quietly. 'It's no use. She's gone.'

'No, no. She can't be,' cried George, his eyes red, tears streaming down his cheeks.

'But her hand?' said Kenny. 'It was so still. She wasn't struggling or splashing. It was like she was waving and it just slipped into the water.'

'I'm sorry, boys' Grandpa Jock said again. 'That's what happens when water enters the lungs. The body stops fighting. It's not like the movies; someone who's drowning won't even be able to cry for help. It's called an instinctive drowning response; she wouldn't even be able to kick her legs.'

'But she can't be gone, Grandpa. I didn't tell her I was sorry,' George buried his head into his elbow. Tears flowed and he gasped for air between sobs.

'I'm so sorry, George.'

George wanted to turn back time; to take back the anger and jealousy he'd shown towards Allison. He felt guilty he was still alive and Allison wasn't. Why had they come to Loch Ness? Why had they come out on a stupid boat?

'We'll have to head into shore and report this to the police,' sighed Grandpa Jock. 'And they'll have to tell her parents too.' Hamish nodded and started to pull the chord. Grandpa Jock shook his head.

'Don't start the engine, lad. I couldn't bare the noise,' said Grandpa Jock softly as he rubbed his eyes. 'Anyway, we're close enough to row to shore.'

Grandpa Jock dipped the oars into the water and pulled back on them. Kenny sat still and silent. George had stopped crying and was breathing heavily.

Breathing. He was lucky to be breathing, he thought. Allison wasn't breathing. The pain in his chest clawed at his heart and tugged a knot from his stomach.

George thought about her death. He could think of nothing else. A cold, silent death, forcing air from her lungs and suffocating her beneath the water.

'Why? Why did she have to die?' shouted George, to no one in particular. 'Why couldn't I have said sorry sooner?'

'George, don't punish yourself. It's not your fault,' said Kenny, reaching out to his friend.

George snapped. 'I know it's not my fault! You butted her with your head when you jumped. You probably knocked her into the water yourself!'

'That's not what happened, George. It was an accident,' said Hamish, trying to defuse the situation.

'AND YOU! Coming out here without life jackets! In your stupid little boat. You're just as much to blame!' George was bright red in the face as he vented his anger. 'You're as much to blame as me!'

Hamish just bowed his head and said nothing. George was angrier with himself but just wanted to lash out, hoping to release the pain inside him. It didn't make him feel better though. He felt worse. He was hurting his friends now, trying to push out his own guilt as he knew his heart was breaking in a way he could never have imagined.

Grandpa Jock tucked the oars inside the boat, stepped over the centre board and sat down beside George. He put his arm around his grandson's shoulder and held him.

The rowing boat gently bumped up against the shoreline and bobbed there with each soft ripple of wave. Nobody wanted to move.

Chapter 18 – Out the Water

George had sat on the pebble beach at the edge of Loch Ness for what seemed like an eternity. Time hadn't stopped; it just had no meaning anymore. The world was an echo of itself; hollow and dull, futile and empty. The knot of pain pressed high in George's chest, crushing his ribs and strangling his breath. Nothing he did could take away the hurt.

The little bay, close to Cherry Island, sat at the foot of a high hill and was surrounded by trees. It was an empty desolate spot and none of their mobile phones were picking up a signal. Walking into Fort Augustus or stopping a car seemed to be the only way to raise the alarm. But the road was quiet and the village was some distance away.

It was way past midnight as Hamish and Kenny began dragging the rowing boat out of the water whilst Grandpa Jock had walked off towards the main road, hoping to flag down a passing car.

George was lost in his thoughts. Allison had been his best friend in Little Pumpington for over a year, at times he felt she was his only friend. She'd been there when he needed her the most and she'd helped him out of some tricky situations. George hated himself for putting up barriers between them recently.

Hamish and Kenny walked across the stony beach, their feet crunching on the pebbles. The only other sound was the ripple of water as it lapped on the shore. They sat down beside George and stared out at the black water.

'I'm sorry, you guys,' said George, breaking the silence. 'I shouldn't have lost it with you both.'

'No worries, mate,' said Kenny. 'I understand.'

'Aye, someone close dying like that can do funny things to your head,' sighed Hamish. 'It's not your fault and we're with you, man.'

There was a stumbling, scuffing sound and a voice cried out from the darkness.

'Ooh ya beggar!' followed by a string of expletives that shattered the still night-time air.

'Aah ya %&*@##!!!@#!'

Seconds later, Grandpa Jock came staggering down from the trees, clutching his elbow.

'Sorry lads, I fell climbing over those logs back there,' he exclaimed. 'Luckily my inflatable pants broke my fall a bit but I've given myself a right sore one.'

George smiled. Even at the most sombre moments Grandpa Jock could always be counted on to ruin the occasion. Last year during the Queen's Christmas speech on TV Grandpa Jock managed to drop the biggest, eggy pump that stunk out the whole house so much George's mum had to opened all the windows, even though it was snowing outside. Silent, but violent, George had called it.

Then there was that time during the two minutes silence on Remembrance Sunday when Grandpa Jock tried to squeeze out another quiet one but only succeeded in letting rip with one of the loudest, proudest bottom burps that George had ever heard. Grandpa Jock said it wasn't disrespectful, it was just wind and his old army mates would be wetting themselves in the graves with laughter at that one.

The more George thought about it, the more he realised that Grandpa Jock loved life. He embraced everything about it, he threw himself into every challenge wholeheartedly, sometimes stupidly, sometimes recklessly but somehow always with as much enthusiasm and honesty as his spirit could carry.

But that wouldn't bring Allison back and going out on

17

Loch Ness in the middle of the night in a tiny little rowing boat and no life jackets was a pretty idiotic thing to do. Grandpa Jock should've known better. We all should've known better, thought George.

The gloomy silence returned to the beach once more and all four of them sat staring out over the water, still not knowing what to do for the best. A trek to Fort Augustus seemed the only option left but the adrenalin that had coursed through their veins during the night's earlier activities was now dragging them down into listless exhaustion.

But Grandpa Jock's fight with the fallen tree, and subsequent swearing had snapped Kenny and Hamish out of their mindless depression; they'd begun to reconsider earlier events and now the unspoken question was floating around the beach like a giant elephant tip-toeing across the pebbles – everybody knew it was there but nobody wanted to mention it.

It was more than Kenny could bear.

'What hit the boat?' he asked.

'What?' said George, the question pulling him back from the pit of despair.

'The boat,' said Kenny again. 'Something hit the boat three times, before Allison… before… she, before….'

The words choked in his throat but Hamish was thinking the same thing and Kenny had now opened that box. The thought was out there.

'There was something in the water,' nodded Hamish. 'We all saw it. There was a creature in the water. It hit our boat.'

'Aye, but nobody would believe us if we told them, lad,' sighed Grandpa Jock. 'So let's not tarnish that lassie's memory with ridiculous talk about monsters and sea serpents, eh.'

Silence hit the beach again.

Chapter 19 – Dog Island

Metal clanged against metal. A steel hatch door slammed against the bulkhead frame and there was a screeching, scraping noise as the locking wheel secured the seal again.

The bunk room was cramped yet only one bed was down. The other three were folded away, flat against the walls. Commander Chuck Choppers stepped in through the hatch with a bundle of dry clothes in his arms.

'We got lots of dry clothes on-board but I'm not sure if any of them will fit you, Miss. This is the best we can do for the moment.' His voice a high pitched Texan drawl.

Allison sat on the bunk, wrapped in warm blankets with her wet hair hanging limply against her face. In her hands she was grateful for the mug of hot chocolate and the four marshmallows that were now fluffing up on top. She smiled and sipped the sweet milky drink.

'Professor Spicer will want to debrief you, you know, on what you witnessed out there tonight, once you're good and ready, Miss.' He winked at Allison. 'But don't worry about him; Marmaduke is a pussy cat really. You can call him Marmy.'

Commander Choppers set the clothes down on the edge of the bunk and retired gracefully, casually saluting to Allison as he left.

Allison took another sip of her hot chocolate and felt the warmth soothe around her body. She was still coming to terms with what had happened in the last few minutes.

She remembered seeing a shape in the water; a fin or a flipper, she was sure about that. Then the bump on the boat had knocked her off balance and she fell into the water. She saw the look on George's face as she plunged backwards into the water; he was terrified. He'd tried to grab her but she was falling too fast. He'd be worried now.

Then, into the darkness she recalled spinning, or being spun. She was nudged and bounced and pushed along under the water. Gentle nudges, not harmful or threatening; more playful than anything else.

She remembered being bounced upwards and bursting to the surface, just enough time to take a breath before her foot was pulled back down into the depths. Faces swam right up to hers. One small pink head, no bigger than her own pressed itself against her forehead. Eyes, cheeky mouth, big pink tongue, wide nostrils, inspecting her, examining her, tasting her... sniffing her?

And with a flick and a swish of tails and flippers, all the creatures disappeared. Her feet were pulled harder and two hands grabbed her around her shoulders. She was thrust down into a metal tube, tight, cramped and confined. She held her breath, terrified to breathe, yet her lungs were bursting; they were on fire and she closed her eyes, hoping for some release from the pain.

A rubber tube was forced into her mouth and she opened her eyes wide with fear. Two eyes stared at her and the face in the mask nodded. Allison drew in the air from the tanks, strapped onto the diver's back. The diver smiled calmly and gave her the thumbs up.

He motioned to her to take another deep breath and he pulled the mouthpiece away from her, taking in lungfuls of air himself. He slipped the breathing tube back into her mouth and pulled the hatch down above them. He swivelled the locking wheel to secure the airlock and pulled down on the flush handle.

Allison's feet hit the deck as the water was expelled from the tube. The diver took off his mask and pulled the air tube from Allison's mouth. Her knees buckled but he caught her before she could fall, not that there was any space to fall into. A second airlock opened and the diver, who she discovered later, was called Chuck Choppers, carried Allison into the main docking bay of the small submarine.

Towels, blankets and hot chocolate followed soon afterwards.

Finishing her drink, she dressed quickly, folding the legs of the long trousers up and turning the sleeves back. The clothes didn't belong to a big man but they still swamped Allison's small frame. She used her own belt to hold the baggy trousers up. She stepped out of the bunk room, along the small corridor and stopped at the hatchway to the cockpit at the front of the vessel.

The three science geeks from the porridge competition were gathered around several monitors on the far wall. Sonar machines bleeped, radars blipped and the thermal imaging cameras flashed the red and yellow hot spots of several large creatures. The thinnest scientist turned around when he heard Allison enter the room.

'Hey, the little mermaid has surfaced,' said Peewee Peterson, in a well-educated American accent. 'How you doing, sweetheart?'

'You're one lucky lady, princess' added Chuck Choppers, 'I wouldn't advise going swimming out there in daylight, never mind in the middle of the night.'

'I wasn't......swimming,' said Allison hesitantly, her jaw beginning to drop, 'I fell overboard.'

'Well, I suppose swimming is the best thing you can do in those circumstances,' replied Chuck.

Allison stared in amazement. From the front of the bridge she saw a huge glass dome stretch up and over the whole room. Beyond, the water was so dark and murky that any visibility was impossible. Occasionally a small fish would swim close enough to the glass to be seen before darting away into the gloom.

'Is this a...' Allison stammered. She paused and took on-

board her surroundings. 'Is this a submarine?'

'Welcome aboard the MIR-CAT, young lady.' Professor Spicer reached out to shake her hand which Allison took tentatively. 'Submarine doesn't do this baby justice. This, my dear, is a self-propelled, pioneering research submersible. My name is Professor Marmaduke Spicer, this is the commander of the vehicle, Chuck Choppers, but you've already met him. And last but not least, Dr Peterson but you can call him Peewee.'

'What is this place?' asked Allison, losing her shyness as she stared around at all the equipment.

The professor rubbed his hand across the wall and felt the energy humming from the reactor. 'MIR is Russian for peace and they designed her. CAT stands for Civilian Aquatic Turbo-reactor. It's basically a research vessel and is one of only seven manned submersibles in the world that can dive beyond 3000 metres.'

'Not that we need to dive to that depth here,' Commander Chuck laughed.

'Loch Ness is only 230 metres deep, which is tremendous for a loch or lake but nothing compared to the ocean beyond. But, as you can see,' the professor waved at the black Perspex window, 'normal visibility is useless, even when we switch on the search lights but we have enough equipment, radar, sonar and thermal to know what's going on around us. We've been using Dog Island as a base to moor the sub; it's sunken below the surface so no one knows we're here.'

Allison wasn't sure if Professor Spicer was talking directly to her or was just in love with his submarine but either way she didn't want to interrupt.

'They discovered the Titanic in one of these babies. The Russians even used one to plant a flag on the seabed at the North Pole, 4000 metres beneath the ice-cap. I bought this one from a bankrupt Ukrainian science academy.'

'But why is it here in Loch Ness, Professor Spicer?' asked Allison, feeling braver now.

'Call me Marmy, it's short for Marmaduke.' Allison got the feeling that the professor was trying to avoid her question.

'Thank you, Marmy but why Loch Ness? What are you looking for?' Allison wasn't going to let it go.

'We've detected some....er unusual seismic activity in this area.' Marmy hesitated. 'This mission is to investigate the fault lines around the Great Glen running through Scotland.'

'You see, some time ago we identified a geographical phenomenon that caused a shifting of the tectonic plates beneath Scotland which affected the subsurface hydrogeology,' Peewee Peterson felt the need to elaborate.

'Does he always speak like that?' asked Allison, glancing between Marmy and Chuck.

'Pretty much, you kinda have to get used to him,' chirped Chuck. 'Peewee is our resident geologist.'

'And Hydrologist. I study water too,' added Peewee.

'Basically, the earth's crust shifted and opened up underground channels. Water started flowing in the opposite direction,' said Marmy, pointing to a map of Scotland and imitating a surface shift with his hands.

'But what are those creatures swimming around out there?' Allison neatly brought the subject back to biology.

'Yeah...' droned Marmy, hesitating again, 'I don't think we can cover that one up for much longer, boys.'

Chapter 20 – The Loch Ness Monsters

The water was flat and calm, dark against the hills beyond and the starry sky above. George, Grandpa Jock, Kenny and Hamish stared out in silence at the blackness. They'd been quiet for a while now and not a single car had passed on the road behind them.

Hamish saw it first. One big bubble bursting on the surface of the water. Then another, and another, followed by a stream of tiny bubbles fizzing out of the loch. Grandpa Jock, Kenny and George had now seen this as well, heard it too as the water began to boil and gurgle.

A sleek, shiny shell seemed to rise out of the water about twenty metres from the shore and it was coming closer. As much as Grandpa Jock didn't want to talk about mysterious creatures, their first thoughts were of the Loch Ness Monster returning to finish them off, just as it had dragged Allison to her doom. The boys staggered to their feet, not taking their eyes off the strange apparition. Grandpa Jock took longer to stand up, his old knees cracking as he did so.

The hull was black and sparkled as the water ran off it. Ten metres now and it was clear to everyone that this was not some water beast come to devour them but something man-made, something solid, something reaching out of the water…

And Allison was waving at them.

Hamish absent-mindedly waved back, not believing what his eyes were telling him. George, Kenny and Grandpa Jock stood and stared.

Allison was smiling and waving at them.

The vision still didn't register. Were they dreaming?

'Allison?' said George, scared to breathe her name in case his dream burst.

Allison was rising up out of the water, smiling and waving at them, surrounded by the science geeks.

'ALLISON!' George yelled, leaping and pointing. Kenny hugged Hamish. Tears filled George's eyes again.

'She's alive!' shouted Grandpa Jock and he grabbed George around the waist. They all began to dance around the beach, still facing the submarine, not daring to take their eyes off the craft.

'Allison's alive. Allison's alive,' sang Hamish and Kenny, their voices filled with relief, joy and pure elation.

George hesitated... And she's in... a submarine?'

Kenny laughed and pointed, 'A submarine!'

Hamish grinned, 'Aye, that's a submarine alright.'

'We all live in a yellow submarine, a yellow submarine' sang Grandpa Jock now, not actually caring that the research submersible was black, without even a hint of yellow on it. He wasn't going to let minor details like that spoil a good sing-song.

'What's she doing in a submarine?' asked George.

'Who cares? She's alive and kicking... in a submarine,' Kenny replied.

But in that split second Allison was gone again. She'd disappeared from view, the scientists too and the boys stopped dancing. Fear took hold. Had it been a hallucination?

The next moment a hatch opened on top of the vehicle and Allison's head popped up.

'George! Mr Jock!' she screamed. 'You'll never believe what I've just seen!'

Right then, George and his Grandpa Jock were willing to believe anything.

It had taken Chuck a few seconds to blow up an inflatable dinghy, using a Rapid-pump Air Blaster contraption on the roof of the sub. He'd launched the dinghy overboard and paddled to the shore to pick up Grandpa Jock and George and returned with them to the submersible. Then he went back to the beach to collect Hamish and Kenny.

Peewee Peterson helped George down the ladder from the hatch into the submarine and George threw his arms around Allison. She looked surprised.

'We thought you were… ' George was filling up again. 'I'm sorry. Sorry for being mean, sorry for being jealous and petty and…'

Allison pulled herself out of George's arms and put her finger over his lips.

'It doesn't matter,' she whispered.

'Aye, I think we've all learned a lesson tonight,' said Grandpa Jock hopping down off the ladder, his now almost-deflated whoopee cushions bouncing around his bum cheeks beneath his kilt.

'You've got to see this, George. It's amazing.'

Professor Spicer stepped out from the cockpit and strode across the deck, holding a large wad of papers. 'Before you say anything, young lady, these gentlemen will need to sign a copy of the Official Secrets Act. What is about to be revealed to you must remain top secret. You cannot discuss these revelations with anyone.'

'I'm not so sure about signing no top secret documents,' muttered Grandpa Jock suspiciously. 'Strange things can happen when officialdom takes over. I remember when I was in Roswell, New Mexico in 1947…'

'Oh, just sign it, Mr Jock. I promise it will be worth it,' urged Allison. 'Oh, and by the way, this is Marmy.'

'Pleased to meet you, Marmy,' said Grandpa Jock, eyeing him up and down cynically. Grandpa Jock snatched up the

28

pen and papers from the professor, muttering 'This had better be good.' He scrawled his signature across the page.

Kenny, then Hamish jumped down the ladder and were followed by Commander Choppers who pulled and locked the hatch down after himself. He stepped through the crowd standing in the passageway and went into the cockpit.

A couple of seconds later George felt the submarine lurch forwards and begin to sink beneath the surface of the water again.

They were all standing in the crowded cockpit as the submarine sailed through the murky water. George reckoned that visibility must've been about two inches.

It took the scientists over twenty minutes to explain the whole truth to the boys. Peewee Peterson demonstrated his earth crust displacement theories on a computer screen. Commander Chuck had shown them photographs, thermal images and sonar traces of several large creatures and Professor Marmy had explained the historic and prehistoric relevance of their discoveries.

George, Hamish and Kenny sat shocked and slack-jawed at what they'd heard. Allison smiled at their astonishment since she'd had time to come to terms with the incredible truth.

Only Grandpa Jock's eyes sparkled with intrigue and imagination.

'So,' he began. 'Let me get this straight. You're telling me that the Loch Ness Monster exists.'

Marmy smiled back and nodded.

'And there's not just one creature but dozens of them, perhaps hundreds living beneath the hills and mountains of Scotland, swimming around in underground rivers.'

'Not just Scotland, Mr Jock,' Allison added. 'But all round Britain.'

'And all over the planet, ma'am,' said Chuck.

'We have reason to believe, sir,' Peewee continued. 'That these underground channels are connected all around the world, linking lakes to seas, lochs to oceans. They were carved millions of years ago by water and ice, through mountains and solid rock.'

'You see, these creatures can survive in both fresh water and sea water and they've been around for centuries. We understand from our examinations that they are a warm-blooded species related to and evolved from the ancient plesiosaurs from the late Triassic period,' added Marmy.

'Some dolphins, turtles and crocodiles can do the same thing, surviving in both salt and fresh water environments.' Chuck butted in.

'OK, I get that bit, the salt water and stuff,' flustered Grandpa Jock. 'But what's all this nonsense about these beasties swimming all over the world?'

'Oh, Mr Jock, weren't you listening?' Allison was becoming agitated. She heard this story twice and was quite convinced by now. 'There are tunnels and caverns plunging into the depths of the earth. They're all flooded, most of the time and the monsters use them to swim to warmer waters in the winter.'

'Excuse me, ma'am.' Marmy had to step in. 'We prefer to call the creatures 'plesiosaurs' or 'sea serpents'. Monsters kinda conjures up a negative stereotype.'

'And remember, they only swim to slightly warmer waters in the winter, not tropical,' Peewee jumped onto his specialist subject. 'We believe the low ambient temperature of Loch Ness is suitable most of the year but fractionally warmer waters in North America are preferable in the winter.'

'Hang on, hang on, hang on. I'm getting a bit lost.' Grandpa Jock shook his head. 'These beasties have been seen in other places?'

'Well, sir,' Marmy went on. 'To start with, in other lochs nearer to home. Here, in Scotland, there is the lesser known legend of Morag, a creature reported to live in Loch Morar, not far from here. After Nessie, Morag is among the best known of Scotland's legends.'

Chuck Choppers was waiting for this bit. He was eager to become involved, 'I love this part,' he said. 'Morag sightings date back to 1887 and include some thirty-four recorded incidents. In 1998 a serpent-like creature six metres long was reported by nine people in a boat, in the same place as the 1887 sighting.'

'And that's only in Scotland,' Marmy added. 'In Okanagan Lake in British Columbia, Canada, locals have reported a lake demon there since the early 19th Century. They've nicknamed it Ogopogo and it is believed to be a many humped variety of sea serpent, about 12 -15 metres long.'

'Ogo-pogo,' George whispered under his breath.

'There are examples like this all around the globe, sir.' Marmaduke hoped his audience would be convinced.

'Right, I know I'm a bit slow, just give me time,' Grandpa Jock closed his eyes and pondered on this new information for a few second. Hamish and Kenny still sat with their mouths agape. Grandpa Jock snapped his eyes open and stared directly at the professor.

'How do they breathe, these plesiosaurs?' Grandpa Jock spoke with confidence and conviction. 'You said they were warm blooded, like dolphins and whales. They'd have to surface regularly as mammals to breathe, so we should have more sightings of them.'

Chuck Choppers nodded. 'They are warm-blooded and yes, they do need to surface regularly... but they do it inside the caverns and tunnels under the mountains. And, like whales, they can stay submerged for over an hour without taking a breath, so when they swim around Loch Ness, they generally keep under the water.'

'OK, I'll give you that,' Grandpa Jock was leading up to his trump card. 'What do they eat? There's fish in Loch Ness but not enough. So what do they eat when they stay here?'

'At first we weren't sure,' admitted Marmaduke. 'Of course they can feed out at sea, but the creatures live here in Loch Ness for months on end.'

'Then, by luck,' Chuck butted in again. 'We discovered that these old passageways are also the ancient migratory salmon routes when the fish travel back to their breeding grounds. Millions of salmon swim through here every year.'

'Hence, there's an unlimited supply of lunch for the peckish plesiosaurs inside the caverns,' smiled Marmaduke.

'And that's where we're headed now,' added Choppers.

Chapter 21 – Into the Caverns

The submarine ploughed through the loch at an impressive twenty knots per hour. It didn't take long before the mouth of the cavern opened up wide on the radar.

George, Kenny, Hamish and Allison stared at the black screen with the green bleeping tracer as it circled the environment around them. Chuck drew a line with his finger through an open channel in the mountainside.

'This is the underground entrance to the caverns,' explained Choppers. 'It's submerged and was partially blocked by rocks in the recent underground earthquake. We can tell it's the opening we're looking for because of the rocky outcrop to the south of the entrance.'

Grandpa Jock stared at the screen, then straight ahead. Allison slapped Kenny's hand; he'd started to pick his nose again.

'It's just nerves,' Kenny whispered.

'It's just disgusting,' replied Allison.

'Only the smallest plesiosaurs can make it out into the loch these days,' added Marmaduke, ignoring Kenny and Allison. 'The rock falls have narrowed the entrance considerably. It's just wide enough for the sub to fit into.'

George felt himself breathe in as the little sub squeezed through the slim passageway. There was a screeching, scraping sound as one side of the sub dragged across the rock wall.

'The passageway has narrowed again, sir,' Choppers reported and Professor Marmaduke nodded.

'That's a worrying development, gentlemen. We must investigate this further, and quickly.'

'We'll need to be careful coming out again,' Peewee confirmed. 'Another small earth shift and we could be trapped in here.'

Allison looked at George, who looked at Kenny, who gulped.

The submersible began to rise out the water in the darkness of the cave. Trails of liquid rolled down the glass and Marmaduke threw down a large lever which activated the external lights. The cavern burst into colour as the strong beams illuminated the vast grotto beyond.

George nearly wet himself when he saw six long, dark necks and tiny heads wavering above the water. The necks stretched five metres high and the serpents blinked in the sharp beams.

Professor Marmaduke stretched out his hands. 'Ladies and gentlemen, I give you the Loch Ness Monster.'

'Or rather 'monsters' – plural, sir,' blurted out Commander Chuck.

'I thought 'monsters' was politically incorrect terminology, professor,' added Allison.

The professor laughed. 'I think the modern phraseology works rather well at this moment of revelation... when the monsters are clearly no longer myths'

Allison nudged George. 'Don't worry, you get used to the way they speak.'

George didn't respond. He was too busy staring out of the Perspex bubble. Kenny, Hamish and Grandpa Jock also stood open-mouthed at the wondrous spectacle before them.

The huge beasts seemed unperturbed by the light and swam gently around the cavern. Several smaller plesiosaurs dived and splashed across the surface, bobbing in and out of the water and playing around the sub. The younger creatures were lighter in colour than the larger mammals.

Grandpa Jock was trying to count them but he couldn't see them all at once, some in, some out of the water. 'Sixteen, seventeen. No, sixteen. Wait, that one's seventeen. Ach, I've lost count again,' he grumbled and began pointing with his finger again.

Hamish was staring at the heat-seeker screen. Orange serpent-like shapes swam all around the submarine on the screen, their body heat glowing on the monitor.

'There're loads of them under the water,' shouted Hamish, pointing at the screen.

'There's a load out here too,' yelled George pressing his face against the Perspex. The enormous cavern reached back as far as the beam of light allowed. George couldn't tell how deep it went into the mountain side. It seemed like every metre of water rippled with wriggling prehistoric bodies.

'Aargh!' George jumped back with fright. An enormous dark head had risen right in front of the glass and was now staring into the cabin. Its yellow eyes sparkled with curiosity as its pupils contracted to tiny pin pricks of black, adjusting to the light in the cockpit.

The large plesiosaur's nostrils flared and blew jets of water vapour across the glass, steaming up the window for a second. George laughed as the dinosaur snot splattered onto the Perspex.

'Urgh!' gasped Allison.

'Great,' giggled Kenny. 'Brontosaurus bogies!'

Professor Spicer laughed. 'You're not far from the truth, young man,' he said. 'We actually believe that this is a hybrid variety of aquatic creature and they can certainly grow as big as a brontosaurus.'

'They all seem very friendly,' Grandpa Jock said soundly, suddenly at peace with the idea that a species millions of years old was living in his midst.

'That's correct, sir,' Commander Choppers replied. 'They live in family groups here in the tunnels and display a calm confidence in this, their natural habitat.'

'It's only when they are out on the loch that they demonstrate any suspicion or timid behaviour,' added Marmy.

'I'm not surprised,' replied Grandpa Jock. 'Camera-crews, big game hunters and poachers have been searching these creatures for years, hoping to make their fortunes.

'They must've scared them off enough times to make the beasties more than a wee bit cautious.'

'And we believe that we are close to understanding the reason for the water shortages in England. This may be the centre of activity,' declared Professor Marmaduke Spicer with the aplomb of an actor on stage.

'You mean, these Nessies is responsible for the drought?' gasped Allison. This was news to her.

'Nessie drank Little Lake Pump?' asked Kenny, a little absent-mindedly.

'No,' replied Peewee. 'But we can connect the two. That's how we first began to realise what we were on to.'

'Now, would you like to explore the tunnels with us?' the professor announced.

'Yeah,' shouted George, Allison and Kenny together.

'No!' screamed Grandpa Jock and Hamish.

'I can't. Angus doesn't know I'm away. If he discovers I'm missing from my bed he'll call the police.' Hamish shook his head. 'I'd be in big trouble.'

'And the Porridge World Championships have been rearranged again for tomorrow, well, today now,' said Grandpa Jock looking at his watch. 'It's almost morning.'

'Oh, come on Grandpa,' insisted George, 'Let's explore the caves.'

'I'd love to, lad but I need to get my secret recipe cooking,' said Grandpa Jock. 'I'm not letting some sneaky saboteur get near my pots this time.'

Commander Chuck Choppers stepped forward. 'It looks like we've got ourselves an old-fashioned Mexican stand-off, folks.' Marmy was first to flinch.

'I tell you what we can do,' said the professor sharply. 'If we're real quick we can get back across to the main harbour before they start pouring all them porridge oats into it. Then we can get back here to check out the problem with these tunnels.'

'And Mr Jock, sir,' Marmy stretched his hand out towards the old Scotsman. 'We'd appreciate if you'd announce our withdrawal from the competition. This situation is becoming serious.'

'It's not dangerous, is it?' asked Grandpa Jock, his ginger brows furrowing. 'I can't let the children go with you if it's too risky.'

'We'll be okay,' nodded Marmaduke. 'We don't expect another land shift for years.'

Chapter 22 – Into the Tunnels

The submarine had squeezed through the tight opening from the caverns back into Loch Ness and shot across the one and half miles' width stretch of water in record time. Dawn was gently breaking and the daylight was just beginning to creep over the mountains as the sub emerged in the harbour and dropped off Grandpa Jock and Hamish on the dock. They waved forlornly towards the craft, as it slipped safely through the gates again.

'I've got my phone... if you need me, George,' Grandpa Jock shouted out across the empty loch as the submersible disappeared beneath the surface and bubbles rose up from the depths.

When they reached the hidden entrance to the caverns once more George was certain that the scraping noise against the sides of the submarine was louder this time. Commander Chuck and Professor Marmaduke exchanged glances as they passed through the narrow channel but didn't say anything.

The sub sailed on through the massive cavern, largely ignored by the plesiosaurs and headed towards the rear of the cave. Staying below the water, some of the young serpents dived and swam around the submersible but soon lost interest when they realised the sub didn't want to play.

Under the water the Perspex dome was pitch black; George, Allison and Kenny could see nothing in the darkness so they sat in the control room watching Choppers navigate the craft using the sophisticated sonar equipment surrounding them. The computers blipped and bleeped and the sub began to dive deeper into the depths.

George felt the sub slow to a crawl as the little green tracer pinged and a large opening appeared electronically at the base of the wall of the cavern.

The commander carefully guided the sub towards the tunnel and they entered a long, straight passageway.

'We can go a little faster here,' admitted Chuck, 'since this tunnel is much wider than the rest. We've mapped out a fair degree of these channels.'

'Just one little rise to negotiate and we'll be there,' confirmed Professor Marmaduke.

'Where is 'there', exactly professor?' quizzed Allison, her eyes narrowing.

'We call it the Grand Canyon,' smiled Marmy. 'It's the focal point for all the seismic activity in the area and Grand Central Station for all the converging passageways.'

George felt the submarine rise up in the water for a few seconds before a scraping noise scratched across the base of the sub.

'Water level at the highest point has decreased again, sir. Zero-point-two metres, sir.' Commander Chuck didn't look up from his sonar screen as he shouted across to the professor.

'Don't worry, boys,' said Spicer winking across. 'That's the highest point of our trip, a little subterranean ledge we need to get up and over to reach the main cavern.'

George stared at Kenny and gulped. The professor sounded confident but that scraping wasn't exactly gentle.

'Dr Peterson?' Allison was addressing Peewee now, the thin scientist with the thick glasses. She'd wanted to call him 'Peewee' but thought it was a bit rude. 'What's the connection between the drought in England and the plesiosaurs? Is it something to do with those seismic shifts you mentioned?'

'My word, the young lady is sharp,' said Peewee, winking over at the professor. 'It had taken us weeks to figure that one out.'

'A little while ago, Britain suffered a minor, yet highly significant land shift,' Peewee explained. 'The whole country is connected by these underground canals and water has been flowing south through these mountains for hundreds of centuries, feeding the lakes of England.'

'After the shift occurred, a massive new fissure opened up in the rock-face, diverting the flow of water to the east, away from England. That's why the lakes dried up.'

'But I could hear water flowing underneath Little Lake Pump last week, so there was some moisture still getting there,' said Allison, thinking back to their trip on the bikes.

'Erm... yes... we'll come back to that one,' coughed Peewee, a little embarrassed.

Just then the submarine began to slow and George felt the craft rise out of the water. The lights outside the sub flashed on and he could see they were in another subterranean cavern, larger than the first, with a high ceiling and black shafts disappearing off in all directions as the canyon stretched away into the darkness.

Immediately to the left of the submarine was a nasty, wide jagged crack running down through the cave banking. Unlike the rest of the walls around the cavern, which were worn and smooth, this split was sharp and raw.

'That's the rupture in the rock-face that was opened recently,' explained Peewee. 'We can tell from the carbon dating readings we took the last time we were in here.'

'Many rivers and tributaries flow into this main cavern. Now all the water seems to flow outwards from this fissure, towards the North Sea and diverts the natural pathway of the water underneath Britain,' said Chuck. 'Originally this cavern would've been totally submerged. See, you can tell from the water line around the roof of the cave.'

'But with the water constantly washing away with the tides,' Peewee stepped in, 'the whole dynamic flow of water has been altered at this point. That's why England's lakes are drying out.'

'These caverns were formed millions of years ago, during the Cretaceous period, carved by ice and worn smooth by water,' added Professor Spicer. 'And we believe that plesiosaurs survived the mass dinosaur extinction 65 million years ago by sheltering down here.'

At that moment a little pink plesiosaur plopped right out of the water and flopped onto a small rocky plateau towards the south of the cavern. There was another tunnel running into darkness behind and as the creature looked over its shoulder, George could've sworn it was laughing at them.

'Maybe you shouldn't look, young lady,' said Peewee trying to cover Allison's eyes with his hand. Allison pulled away and stepped towards the glass. George and Kenny already had their faces pressed up against the window.

The little plesiosaur had turned to face them, dipping its soft fleshy tail into the watery basin with a splash. The tiny creature's mouth tensed and its eyes crossed before a delightful sigh of relief spread over the animal's face. Water splashed up from the pool behind.

'Is... is... is it...' Allison stuttered, 'doing the toilet?' George and Kenny chuckled.

'Yes ma'am,' barked Commander Chuck. 'We believe that all the creatures, not just the young ones like that, defecate and urinate in this area, away from their main living habitat.'

'Well, that's nice,' said Allison. 'They don't want to pee or poop where they swim, so they come out here.'

George and Kenny were now sniggering away uncontrollably.

'What's so funny, you two?' snapped Allison. 'I think that shows some sophisticated behaviour. I mean, when you go to the swimming pool you don't wee in the water, do you?'

George stopped laughing and looked at Kenny. Kenny stopped laughing and stared at George. Then the two of them burst out into a fit of hysterical giggles.

'Urgh, you do! You pee in the pool!' groaned Allison. 'I'm never going swimming with you two again!'

With tears streaming down their faces George and Kenny high-fived each other breathlessly.

'And where... and where does that tunnel lead to?' gasped George, now beginning to put two and two together. The little animal slipped back into the water only to be replaced by another plesiosaur, this time a much larger one.

'We believe that channel flows south, sir' said Chuck, pointing to the sonar map on the screen.

'South? Towards England?' asked George, just to be sure.

'Is that what I heard flowing beneath Little Lake Pump then?' asked Allison, a little tentatively.

'Yes, ma'am, most probably correct, ma'am'

'A river of wee?'

'Yes, ma'am.'

'That's why the soil smelled so bad,' spat Kenny, sniffing at his fingers again to see if they were still stinky.

'Urgh, you were crawling around in it, George,' yakked Allison.

'Well, your face was covered in it!' fired back George, remembering Allison's mud-pack.

'Yes, it's true, kids. There is a strong possibility that you were all rolling around in plesiosaur urine,' laughed the professor. 'But we won't hold that against you.'

Commander Chuck chipped in, 'It hasn't all been flowing south. Some of the wee has been seeping back into Loch Ness too, that's why it's becoming saltier and more acidic. You were probably washing your dishes in it and drinking it as well.'

'And overflowing with plesiosaur pee at low tide,' insisted the professor.

'The question is,' Peewee interrupted. 'How do we repair the rift in this cavern and stem the flow away from the North Sea?'

'And if we can't, England will be drier than a popcorn's fart!'

Chapter 23 – Porridge Part 2

By the time Grandpa Jock and Hamish reached the fair ground and the main marquee all of Drumnadrochit was buzzing with the rumours. Security had been tightened immensely and every part-time policeman from miles around had been drafted in to protect the World Porridge Championships and its competitors. Even firemen had been brought in as additional support for the over-worked police forces in the area.

Laird Baird was standing at the entrance to the marquee and the big, bearded Scotsman welcomed Grandpa Jock with a hearty greeting.

'Morning Jock. Morning Hamish. How are you two doing? Where's the other three?'

'Aye... er... we're fine, we're fine,' said Grandpa Jock, stalling and not sure where the conversation was headed. He didn't exactly wish to discuss where they'd been all night. 'They're... eh... having a bit of a long lie back at the tents.'

'Lazy wee monkeys, eh?' Laird Baird leant in. 'What do you think of the extra security, Jock? We're not taking any chances this time.'

'Aye, very good. Lots of policemen and that, good,' said Grandpa Jock, glad of the change of subject.

'And firemen too, Jock,' boasted the Laird. 'There's a huge fire engine parked around the back of the marquee, next to the oat truck. If the saboteur strikes again we can use the water cannon against him.'

'A bit extreme, don't you think?' mused Grandpa Jock

'Aye, but have ye heard the news, Jock? We've discovered who the saboteur was.' Grandpa Jock raised his bushy eyebrows. Laird Baird shook his head. 'I'd never have believed it unless I'd seen the evidence with my own

45

eyes. He's been planning this for months.'

'Who? Who's been planning it?' asked Hamish, keen to find out more about the biggest scandal ever seen in the small town.

'I still can't get over it myself,' the Laird was scratching his beard and leaning on his stick.

'Who was it?' Grandpa Jock was clenching his false teeth with anticipation.

'Aye, who'd have thought it, eh lad,' nodded Laird Baird. 'He didn't show up for evening service on Sunday night so I went round to his house. It was a wee bit strange because the door was open but he wasn't at home.'

'Who?' asked Grandpa Jock again.

Laird Baird went on. 'But in the kitchen, I found that Reverend McVicars kept a large pile of rabbit poo, a massive stash of salt, a large bottle of vinegar, an industrial size tin of mustard powder, some gunpowder and a jar of extra spicy wasabi paste.

'Wasa wasa, what what?' asked Hamish, in a slightly puzzled way.

'It's a sort of Japanese sauce, lad,' answered Grandpa Jock. 'Tastes like a mixture of raw ginger and menthol mouthwash.'

'Mmmm, sounds braw,' said Hamish sarcastically.

'It's as if he'd vanished,' shrugged Laird Baird, stroking his bristles. 'Apparently McVicars objected to the championships being held on a Sunday, taking the good Lord's name in vain on the Sabbath so he fixed all the porridges with his disgusting concoctions. Then he pretended to be judging the poetry contest all the time.'

'But how did you know it was really the reverend?' argued Grandpa Jock. 'I mean I've got mustard, vinegar and salt in my kitchen too. OK, I don't have rabbit poo but we could stretch the point.'

'I thought of that too,' sighed Laird Baird. 'But when I went into his living room I saw that he'd printed off pictures of all the competitors' faces from the Porridge World Championship website and stuck them all over his wall and he'd... eh... defaced them, shall we say.'

He handed Grandpa Jock a sheet of paper with his smiling photograph on it, the picture he'd sent in with his application. Someone had coloured in one of his teeth black and drawn horns above his head. He had a little goatee beard, a scar, glasses and there was a dagger shoved into his brain with the words 'Die, non-believer, die!' scrawled in red pen across the top.

'There's dozens of pictures like this, throughout the house. Every competitor, as well as yours truly for allowing the competition to go ahead on a Sunday, is included.' Laird Baird shook his head again. 'He's truly insane.'

'But we've beefed up security,' he said pointing at the extra officers. 'And it shouldn't be too difficult to track down a smelly old vicar with a dirty dog collar.'

Laird Baird continued. 'The World Porridge Championships are up for grabs this morning and the men from the Guinness Book of Records will be down at the harbour later for the largest bowl of porridge attempt.'

'Right, young man,' declared Grandpa Jock. 'Let's get cooking!'

Chapter 24 – Stuck!

Back in the cavern Allison sat with her head in her hands, trying to block out the thoughts about drinking sea serpent wee and her mucky mud-pack facial. George and Kenny stood pressed up against the plexi-glass window. The pink plesiosaur they'd seen earlier still swam around the sub, occasionally popping its head up, craving attention.

'That little one's just a baby, we reckon no more than a few months old due to the very light colouration of the skin. We call him Muncher,' Commander Choppers had shouted across from his console. 'He's cute and only two metres long but he could still rip your arm off. I've seen what he can do to the salmon.'

George laughed. 'Yeah, the Loch Ness Muncher.'

The little dinosaur swam around, splashing and playing like a dolphin. At first Muncher was quite cute but the boys soon lost interest as they stared across to the rocky ledge, fascinated to watch a procession of plesiosaurs swim up to their toilet, take a quick leak or dump a big one, then dive back into the water and swim away. The little plesiosaur played on beside the sub.

Kenny was first to break the silence. 'You can't really say that's a quick leak, George, can you? I mean some of those serpents are slashing for Scotland.'

'I noticed that,' replied George, still staring at the animal antics. 'Their bladders must be as big as a bus.'

'Heh heh, I didn't know buses had bladders,' smiled Kenny. Allison moved her hands over her ears.

'Boom boom,' sniggered George.

'During our early tests, we discovered that a plesiosaur's bladder expels about 300 litres of water every day,' laughed the commander. 'They seem to consume a lot of liquid as they swim but it quickly passes through their bodies.'

And just to prove the point another plesiosaur swept out of the water and landed on the pee platform. Instead of dipping its tail into the basin behind, the plesiosaur rolled onto its back. George and Kenny had never seen this behaviour before.

'Chuck, Chuck, what's this one doing?' shouted George.

Commander Choppers turned around from the back of the main cabin, smiling. He enjoyed watching the boys learn more about nature, even if a certain girl was slightly less than impressed.

'That, sir, is a young adolescent male taking on a test of manhood,' nodded Choppers. 'We believe that in plesiosaur society, as in many other creature cultures, young bucks need to prove their strength and bravery through a series of challenges. We think this is one of the earlier trials.'

'Yes, but why is it lying there on its back,' insisted George.

'Just wait and you'll see.'

At that moment a large arc of liquid sprayed out from below the plesiosaur's belly and splattered up the cave wall. The serpent arched its back, splashing the pee higher up the rocks. The urine kept coming, the dinosaur wriggled from side to side, skooshing its wee in a large semi-circle.

Suddenly the fountain lost its power and dripped and drizzled to a halt. The boys watched as an occasion splash splattered into the basin but failed to reach across to the wall. Drained, the dinosaur rolled over onto its tummy and disappeared back into the water. The smallest plesiosaur rose up and out of the water, slapping its two pink flippers together in a show of appreciation.

'We believe that to be one of the first rites of passage for the young plesiosaurs, proving they are big enough and strong enough to take their place alongside the adults,' explained Choppers. 'We think they are trying to wee highest against the wall. The other serpents see or smell the splash marks and decide if the youngster is old enough to join the adult group.'

'Urgh! Boys!' groaned Allison from behind her hands. George and Kenny smiled and high-fived each other again.

Then the submarine began to shake.

Everything on board began to vibrate violently and George felt his teeth shudder. The three youngsters looked at the commander, who grabbed onto the handrail.

'Hold on!' he yelled and everybody reached for the metal railing that ran around the wall of the submersible at waist height.

Small rocks and gravel fell from the ceiling of the cavern and splashed down into the water around the sub. Muncher the baby plesiosaur dived beneath the water. A few pebbles smacked against the Perspex and Kenny prayed the glass was strong enough.

Peewee Peterson and Professor Spicer staggered into the cockpit, fighting to hold their balance. They began pushing buttons and turning dials, in between making frantic grasps on any piece of solid equipment bolted to the floor. A low, growling rumble echoed around the outside of the sub and the whole craft shuddered.

As quickly as it started, the shaking and the noise stopped. The water still splashed against the glass as the waves lapped vigorously outside. George could still feel the tremor in his legs but decided that it was his knees shaking.

'I don't believe it, sir but that was another land shift,' Peterson confirmed, tapping the monitor in front of him.

'The rift has gotten wider, sir,' Choppers pointed to the sonar screen. 'Almost a metre this time.'

'Professor, the water levels are dropping dramatically,' Peterson yelped, aware now that their environment had changed. Something was seriously wrong.

Immediately the professor spat out an order to the

commander. 'Get us out of here, Chuck.'

The commander forced the throttle down. The sub lurched forward and began to sink below the water. Once fully submerged the craft opened up its propellers and surged ahead.

'Sir, do you think... ' Choppers stopped his sentence short.

'We'll soon find out, commander.'

'What is it? What's the matter?' asked George, looking nervously between the two scientists. Kenny backed away into the corner, taking comfort from his forefinger up his nose.

'It's that ridge, professor, isn't it?' asked Allison, sharp and alert, any concern about plesiosaur pee on her face a distant memory.

'Like I said, ma'am, we're about to find out.'

George stepped over to the commander's console and pointed to a bump on the screen. 'That's the ledge there, isn't it?' said George, a statement more than a question.

'Yes, sir, it is.'

'And the water is draining out of this canyon faster than before?'

'That would be an affirmative, sir,' replied Choppers, staring intently at the screen and pressing the throttle hard forward, every inch of his being forcing the sub along faster.

'Are we going to make it?' George looked across to Allison, who'd figured out their plight a few seconds earlier. It was Kenny's turn to block out reality.

'As the professor says, sir, we'll soon find out.'

The submarine rose in the water as they approached the crest of the tunnel. Through the plexi-glass, George and Allison could see the roof of the cavern becoming brighter and brighter as the water became shallower. The sub's light shone beyond the surface of the water, illuminating the ridge above.

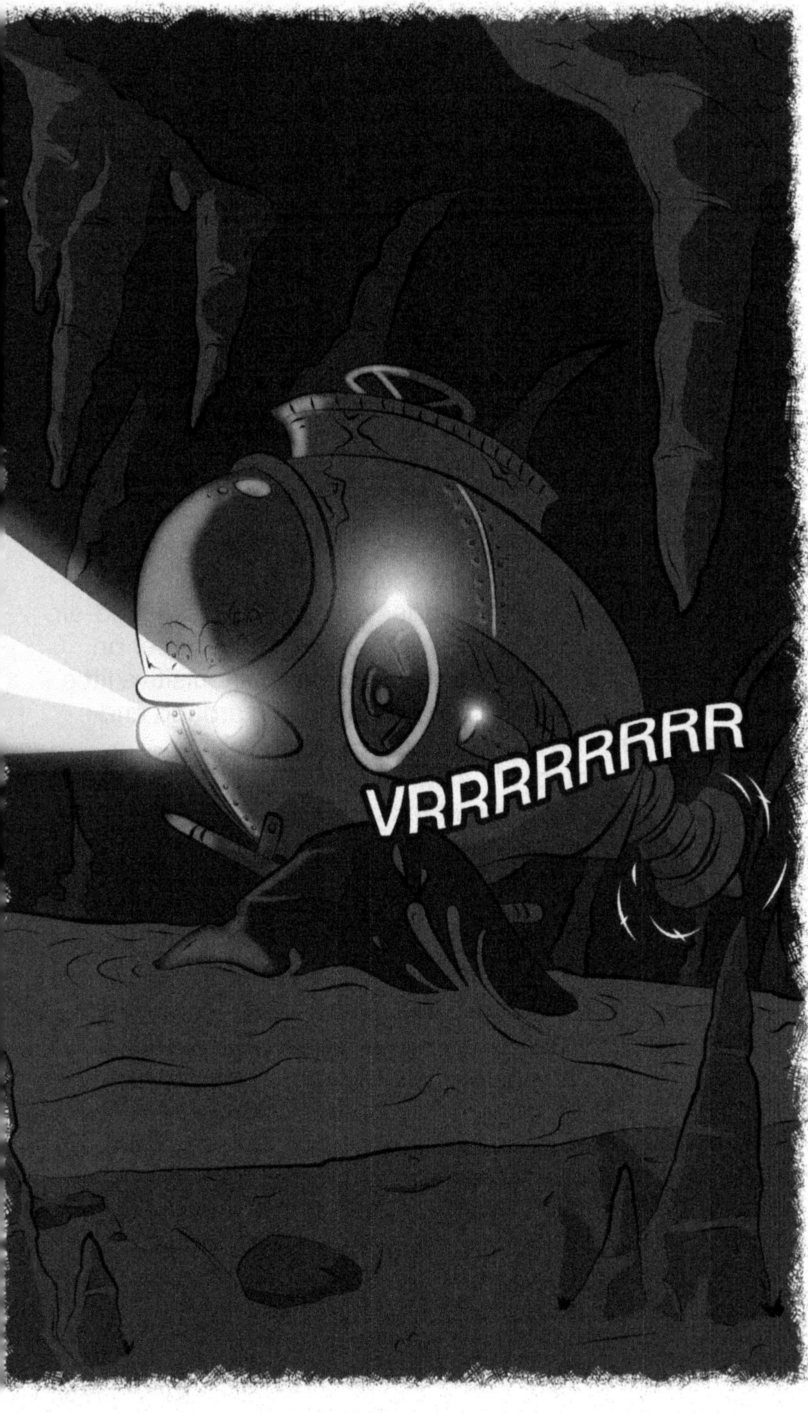
VRRRRRRRRR

The vehicle began to scrape along the bottom on the tunnel and Choppers pushed the throttle forwards.

The sub broke free and leapt out of the water like a seal sailing over the sea for a few moments. Unfortunately, there wasn't enough power and momentum to reach the deep pool on the other side and the craft thudded to a standstill, perched and stranded, neither fully in nor completely out of the water. The tunnel's ledge, that they had sailed over less than an hour before, had drained sufficiently to leave them high and dry.

The craft rocked gently pack and forth on the rocky ledge in a small chamber at the highest point of the tunnel. The three scientists and their young passengers looked into the pool ahead. Down there and along that channel lay Loch Ness and the way out; only they couldn't reach it.

Just then, Muncher splashed up and out of the Grand Canyon pool and over the ridge. With a tiny twist in mid-air, the baby plesiosaur plunged smoothly into the water on the Loch Ness side and within seconds his inquisitive little head was back up out of the water, looking around and wondering why the big sub hadn't followed.

'Could we swim for it?' asked Spicer.

'No sir, we only have one tank of air and that's been partially used,' replied Choppers with a serious look on his face. 'And it's way too far to swim without breathing apparatus.'

Kenny butted in. 'Can't we go back to the Grand Canyon bit?'

The professor stood up but Chuck answered first. 'I'm afraid not, son. Even if we could get off this ledge, the Grand Canyon doesn't lead anywhere. And the sub's too big to squeeze down any of those other tunnels.'

'So, we can't go forward and we can't go back. What are we going to do?' asked George. 'Do you guys have satellite tracking on board or a global positioning system or something?'

'Sorry George,' said Professor Spicer. 'We deactivated those systems when we commissioned the submarine. We didn't want any unwelcome bounty hunters tracking us down.'

'Might be kinda useful now though,' grunted George. 'What about radio communication?'

'No! I refuse to give this location out across the airwaves,' snapped Spicer. 'Every big game hunter, reporter and television crew would descend on this spot from all over the world. Not to mention the million onlookers the creatures would attract. I will not have their habitat destroyed.'

'So we're stuck here then?' asked Allison dolefully.

Chuck Choppers answered in his long Texan drawl. 'Yes, ma'am. We're stuck like a butt in a bucket.'

'Well, just for the next two or three hours,' said Peterson, with a heavy sigh.

'Why? What happens in two or three hours?' George raised an eyebrow.

'The air in this chamber will run out!'

Chapter 25 – Muck!

The World Porridge Making Championships part two was in full swing. Nineteen of the twenty tables in the main marquee were buzzing with activity as the professional chefs whisked up a storm with the passionate, gifted amateurs.

Only the Science Geeks USA table was empty and Grandpa Jock wasn't about to say what they were up to, simply stating to the judging committee that they'd withdrawn.

Actually, buzzing might not be the best way to describe this inner tent action. Panic might be a better description. Pandemonium would be good. But unfettered chaotic bedlam probably sums up the riotous excitement best of all.

Ever since Laird Baird announced that, for this year only, the World Porridge Championships' preparation and cooking time would be reduced from four hours to just two the marquee was afflicted by an outbreak of mass hysteria amongst the participants.

Laird Baird regretted the decision to shorten the Championships but felt he had no choice. The officials from the Guinness Book of Records were coming at 2pm to witness the world's largest bowl of porridge being made. To be more precise about it, the world's largest harbour of porridge. The porridge contest had to be completed soon to allow all the local competitors to take part in the world record attempt. The oatmeal truck was parked around the back of the marquee ready to go.

Chefs are naturally flighty people at the best of times, rising to the top of their profession through a carefully blended mixture of creativity, a desire for perfection and borderline psychopathic tendencies. Having seen their cooking time reduced by half a few of the chefs decided they would cross that border.

Grandpa Jock nudged Hamish and quietly pointed down at table thirteen where the Italian team had started to hit each other with long crispy baguettes. The television crew had spotted the commotion too and had discreetly taken up position at the side of the big tent, filming the events for their 'fly-on-the-wall' documentary.

'Zis eez mook, Luigi,' squealed the fattest Italian chef in an accent so thick you could cut it with a pizza slicer. 'I would not feed zis to my dog!' and he tipped the pot of porridge onto the floor, threw his apron onto the table and stormed out of the tent.

Just to prove him wrong, or to show that Scottish dogs are a little less discerning eaters than Italian hounds, two local strays bolted under the table and began to enjoy the feast. The dogs only stopped eating and decided to make a quick exit when the chefs at table fourteen picked up two large meat cleavers and considered changing their recipe at the last minute.

The Korean team had initially chosen a vegetarian option of Pak Choi Porridge with Five Spice Porridge Powder but with the availability of such fine local ingredients they might've been persuaded to beef up their recipe. Until, that is, they saw the London television crew zooming in for stereotypical close-up, they hid their cleavers behind their backs and began whistling nonchalantly. The dogs didn't even realise they'd been spared.

'Zat eez mook,' said Grandpa Jock in his best Italian accent, 'Zis eez non muck. This is real porridge, lad. Oh, Hamish man, taste that. It's brilliant.'

Grandpa Jock handed the spoon to the ginger haired teenager and his eyes lit up.

'Aye, Mr Jock, that's one of the best porridges I've ever tasted,' confirmed Hamish.

'Right, lad. You keep stirring the honey haggis and I'll start the whisky sauce,' Grandpa Jock felt in charge in the kitchen and reminded him of his army days.

Whilst Grandpa Jock was preparing his sauce intently, Hamish looked up from his stirring. Some spinney, whirly nonsense had caught his eye at the bottom of the tent. Beyond the Italian table, where the irate chefs were still shouting and gesturing at each other, a small girl was performing cartwheels in front of her portable stove. Occasionally she'd jump into the air and throw ingredients into her pot; Hamish nudged Grandpa Jock, who stopped tasting his whisky sauce (for the seventh time) and stared across.

The girl, who must've been about ten years old, was wearing a blue sparkly leotard. Her long brown hair was tied back into a ponytail and this whipped around viciously as she performed a series of twirls and jumps and other gymnastic japery on top of her table.

'You can't cook like that!' gasped Grandpa Jock, dipping his finger into the whisky sauce one more time. 'That's an accident waiting to happen, Hamish lad.'

'Let's go look, Mr Jock,' urged Hamish, and the two of them abandoned their posts to witness the acrobatic madness for themselves. From a distance they could read the competitor sign pinned to the front of the little girl's table. It read 'Marvellous Marcie - Pommel Horse Porridge' and the girl was in the midst of grabbing the handles of her porridge pot and spinning her legs round the table in a criss-cross fashion.

'I see you're impressed by our little gymnast then, Mr Jock,' remarked Laird Baird, as he snuck up behind Grandpa Jock and he nodded across to the girl with his beard. 'Young Miss Landels over there is an excellent acrobat. I do believe she's hoping for extra marks for artistic impression with her porridge.'

'Aye, she's, erm… fairly leaping about there,' stammered Grandpa Jock, wondering if he should try jumping on top of his table for extra marks from the judges.

'I'm a little bit worried about her positioning next the Italians though,' grumbled Laird Baird. 'The poor girl hates cheese and those Italian chappies seem to have rather a lot of it.'

Behind the *Pizza, Pizza* team's table was a stack of mozzarella slabs taller than Grandpa Jock. The Italian chefs were now breaking bits of cheese off and throwing them at the Koreans, who were batting them away with their cleavers. Lumps of cheese were bouncing off Marvellous Marcie, as she balanced on the end of her pot, and some chunks were even landing in her hair.

'This is going to end in trouble,' muttered Grandpa Jock, and he pushed Hamish back towards their table.

'I hope she doesn't fall into her porridge,' added Hamish.

The explosion occurred around the vicinity of table six!!

An Irish-American entrant by the name of Aloysius O'Ween was trying to recreate the classic Thanksgiving dish Pumpkin Pie, substituting the pie part with porridge. Unfortunately, Al, as he was known to his friends, had allowed the pumpkin puree to boil over the edge of the pot and the orange gloop had extinguished the flame.

The oven ring was fixed to a portable gas canister, and without the flammable combustion of the burner the gas continued to seep out of the tank into the air.

It was only when Team India, located next to the Irish-American chef, started to recreate their masterpiece Mutton Dansak with a Whisky Infused Porridge, that they threw two kilos of fiery red chillies and cheap Indian whisky into the hot oil, that some of the searing mixture splashed over the gas canister and ignited.

The resultant fireball singed every moustache and eyebrow in a three metre radius. Luckily the English celebrity chef Heston Bloomingheck was completely untouched, probably because he was totally bald to begin with but the snails for his famous Snail Porridge took a bit of a roasting. Laird Baird was standing on the periphery of the flames and a few flying embers managed to ignite pieces of food that had been lodged in his beard over the last few days. Thankfully Marvellous Marcie was safe but she was now wearing most of her porridge over her leotard, as well as lumps of melted cheese sticking to her hair.

Within moments of the explosion the full-time firemen on duty, acting as part-time policemen for the event, were on the scene, dragging fire blankets from their truck, which was parked around the back of the tent. Quickly, they brought the blaze under control but unfortunately Al O'Ween's pumpkin porridge was ruined and Team India had lost their entire stock of chilli, oatmeal and cheap, yet highly volatile whisky.

As a nation, India loves whisky as much as the Scots but their drink closer resembles paint stripper and thousands of Indians have been known to go blind drinking their evil concoction. Dejected, the Indian team and the entrants at tables four, five and six were forced to withdraw from the competition.

Once the fire chief had established that Laird Baird's beard was not about to burst into flames again, normality returned to the World Porridge Championships tent. Or as close to normality as the north of Scotland can get.

Whilst all this was going on Grandpa Jock fought furiously against the urge to wet himself laughing again as Hamish continued to mix up one delicious pan of honey haggis.

'That's the funniest thing I've seen in ages, man,' chuckled Grandpa Jock, as Laird Baird was led out of the tent by the fire chief, with his combustible beard dipped into a pot of Indian yoghurt.

'You can't take any chances,' the fire chief was muttering to the Laird as they walked by.

At that moment Grandpa Jock's mobile went off. He'd only recently changed his ringtone from the Pipes and Drums of the Royal Dragoon Guards to House of Pain's 'Jump Around' so at first he didn't realise what the noise was; he just carried on stirring his whisky sauce and softly singing 'Jump up, jump up and get down'.

It was Hamish who gave him a nudge and Grandpa Jock flipped the top of his handset and held it to his ear.

'Hullo.'

'You're where?'

'Stuck like a what in a bucket?'

'How long?'

'Who?'

'The Loch Ness Muncher?'

'Right, hang on. I'll be there in a jiffy.'

Grandpa Jock snapped his handset together and shoved his phone into his sporran.

'You take over here, Hamish. I've got some work to do.' And the old Scotsman ran towards the back door of the tent, passing the smoldering tables of pumpkins, porridge and the partially burnt snail shells, as well as a bemused TV camera crew.

Chapter 26 – Duck!

George put his phone back into his pocket.

'He's on his way,' he said to Kenny and Allison, who were alone in the submarine. The scientists had opened the hatch on the roof and had crawled out onto the ridge to weigh up their options.

'But what's he going to do once he gets here?' moaned Kenny. 'No offence to your Grandpa Jock, he is the coolest octogenarian I've ever seen but even he can't swim through the monster filled cavern and that tunnel.'

'He'll think of something,' urged George, hoping his grandpa could conjure up some subterranean surprise. 'Anyway, an octogenarian is someone in their eighties. We don't know how old my grandpa is.'

'Oh George, don't split hairs. We need a miracle or we're all going to suffocate in here,' yelled Kenny, starting to feel the walls closing in around him. He sank quietly into the corner.

'It'll be okay, Kenny,' hushed Allison gently. 'I've seen Grandpa Jock get out of worse fixes that this,' she lied.

'And guys, whilst I think it's very noble that the scientists are putting the welfare of an entire species so high on their priority list,' Allison went on, 'but it's going to be at our expense.'

'Well, if they won't raise the alarm, then I just did,' said George, crossing his fingers for his grandpa.

The three of them sat in silence as they watched the scientists search around outside on the small rocky ledge. The water lapped around their feet as they tried to push the submersible forward. The sub didn't budge an inch. They tried climbing onto the roof and push down with their feet but there was only enough room for the hatch door to open. The scientists could only crawl around without the space to even crouch properly.

All the while Muncher the baby plesiosaur splashed around in the water, curious to see what the men were up to. Eventually the scientists shook their heads with a resigned sense of foreboding and clambered back into the sub.

Commander Chuck was first to slide down the ladders, followed by Peewee Peterson. Professor Marmaduke Spicer was last to enter, pulling the hatch closed behind him and turning the air-lock.

'It's no use out there,' Marmy said, shaking his head. 'The sub is too heavy to push off this ledge, it's too far to swim forwards and there's nowhere to go backwards.'

'Er...we could always radio for help,' suggested Allison tentatively.

'NO! Darn it, I will not compromise the safety of those animals!' barked Spicer. It was the second time he'd lost his cool and the pressure of the moment was getting to him.

'What the professor means is that we'll have to reconsider our other options, kids,' explained Choppers calmly.

'You don't need to patronise us, commander. We're well aware of our situation,' replied Allison.

'And we're smart enough to take steps to fix it,' added George.

'What do you mean?' snapped Spicer, a little alarmed. 'What have you done?'

'I have called my Grandpa Jock and he's coming to our rescue,' said George thrusting out his chest.

'What? No, he's just an old man. How can he help us?' All the various scenarios were running through Spicer's head, permeating out the different computations.

'He has been here before, sir,' confirmed Commander Chuck. 'He's signed the Official Secrets Act, he's aware of the plesiosaurs and the importance of the discovery.'

'But how will he get in here? He can't swim? He can't drag in the equipment needed to block off that rupture.' Marmy Spicer was furious now. 'He'll need to get help and when he does, he'll blow the whole gig wide open.'

'Mr Jock's a clever man. He'll figure something out.' Allison was absolutely certain that Grandpa Jock could solve their dilemma and George could feel himself suddenly filling up with pride in the conviction of his friend.

'Now just you wait a gosh-darn minute, little missy,' Marmy was losing the plot. 'I have a gosh-darn IQ of 229, gosh-diggity-darn it! And I will not believe that some gosh-darned porridge pensioner in a skirt will solve this problem faster than me.'

The raised voices had shaken Kenny of out his petrified state and he jumped in to defend Grandpa Jock's honour, shouting,

'He's got a lot more than a high IQ will get you. Grandpa Jock has a ton of ingenuity and a bucketful of good ol' British brain power. He'll think of something.' Professor Spicer was rocked by Kenny's outburst. The cockpit fell silent.

'And it's a kilt, sir,' George said calmly.

'What?'

'It's not a skirt, it's called a kilt,' snapped Allison, coming to George's defence. 'Come on boys, let's leave the brain boxes to stew in their own juice.' And Allison turned on her heel and marched off the bridge. George and Kenny were quick to follow.

The cavern was only slightly less stuffy than inside the submarine but Allison had hoped that stepping outside would give everyone a chance to settle down. Tempers were frayed, nerves were raw and the situation was becoming more desperate by the minute.

George and Kenny stood at the side of the water and casually kicked stones into the murky depths. They were facing the loch side of their tomb and the pebbles plopped and splashed, causing perfect circles to ripple outwards to the edge of the small cavern. Muncher saw the stones plop into the water and dived in after them.

Allison sat at the bottom of the ladder, lost in thought. The air around them was warm and humid and the lights from the front of the submersible were starting to dim. Splash, splosh, plop went the little stones as George and Kenny tried to distract themselves.

'Of course I'm grateful that he rescued me but he seems to be a little unstable at times.'

'I'm worried about the professor too,' said Allison quietly. 'I know what you mean,' replied George, walking across. 'Did you see the way he stormed out of the main marquee when he realised someone had tampered with his popping space porridge, or whatever it was called.'

'I don't think he's dealing with the pressure very well,' agreed Allison. 'I think he could blow at any moment.'

'Erm, talking about blowing,' groaned Kenny from the water's edge, 'It's been quite a while since I... er... you know, relieved the pressure.' Kenny was now crossing his legs and his face began to turn a delicate shade of red.

'I'm kinda bursting myself Kenny,' agreed George. 'Splashing around in the water didn't help.'

'Oh really, you boys!' sighed Allison, stepping up on the ladder. 'You have bladders the size of peas.'

'A bladder full of pee, maybe,' grunted Kenny, hopping

from side to side, holding the front of his trousers.

'And the size of a football right now too,' added George, realising that toilet talk was a lot like yawning; once one person started, it set everybody else off.

'Enough, already!' called Allison as she reached the top of the ladder and looked down on the two jiggling boys.

'Just hurry up and get inside, would ya!'

'Yeah, give us some privacy!'

Allison stepped down off the ladder inside the submarine, her oversized shirt catching on one of the rungs. She tugged it free and crossed over towards the bunkroom where she'd first woken up on-board. She planned to stay out of the bridge and steer clear of the professor, no matter what mental state he might be in. She just wanted a little time by herself. However, that's easier said than done on a small submarine.

She'd barely set foot into the room when Commander Chuck came in behind her. He reached out to put his hand on her shoulder, then pulled it away. Allison turned.

'Look Miss, I'm sorry about the professor,' shrugged the American. 'He's in the control room now, trying to call for help. He's under a lot of pressure and what with the sabotage and becoming trapped and all...'

Allison looked up, her eyes set firmly at the commander's. He paused.

'He needs to learn some manners,' said Allison firmly, holding her heard high. 'We're only trying to help.'

Before he could answer, a high pitched voice squeaked

through from the bridge. It was Doctor Peewee, who could hardly speak for laughing...

'Chuck, Chuck, you gotta come and see this,' he giggled. 'These two young bucks are having a hissing contest.'

Choppers turned and ran towards the cockpit, closely followed by Allison. Peewee was pressing his face up against the glass and holding his sides.

'They've been at it for almost a minute now and they're still going strong.'

In the cavern, with their backs to the submarine, George and Kenny were peeing high against the wall. Large damp arcs of wee were stretched against the rock and occasionally they'd glance across at each other. Spurred by the height his friend could reach with his wee, the other would stand on his tip-toes and force out a stronger blast of urine, aiming higher than ever.

At one point Kenny tried to jump and wee against the wall at the same time but only succeeded in covering his hands in pee. He shook off the splashes and tidied himself up. George was dribbling to a finish.

'Perhaps you shouldn't be watching this, Miss?' Chuck suggested, with a wry smile.

'Oh I'm not watching them, Commander,' smiled Allison, pointing across at the water. 'But I think Muncher is.'

Both Peewee and Chuck turned to see a small pink head watching the boys with interest, his nostrils twitching in the air. Then with a silent swish of his tail the little plesiosaur dipped below the surface.

'Uh oh, I've seen this behaviour before... through in the other cavern,' spat Peewee. 'It's that dinosaur test of manhood ritual that they do.... Oh no boys, DUCK!'

It's doubtful if the boys would've been able to hear Doctor Peterson shouting from the inside of the plexi-glass. They certainly heard the splash of the plesiosaur as it rose up out of the water. The creature sailed through the air gracefully and George and Kenny stared, open-mouthed in amazement.

Then, as if to join in their weeing contest, the plesiosaur unleashed an enormous spray of pee, splashing over the wall, the beach and the boys. Steam rose up from where the urine splashed down and the playful young dinosaur dipped below the water once more. George and Kenny were soaked!

Once Chuck and Peewee had stopped laughing, the commander stood up and stepped towards the door of the cockpit.

'Looks like we're gonna need more of them dry clothes after all!'

Even with the hatch left wide open the air inside the submarine felt warm and stuffy. This wasn't helped by the steaming pile of serpent-pee soaked clothes heaped in the corner of the cockpit. George and Kenny sat sheepishly on the bridge sipping their mugs of hot chocolate, draped in their oversized outfits. Even the air was beginning to taste stale and this had nothing to do with the bad taste left in their mouths. The oxygen in the cavern was running low.

They'd turned the lights off to save the submersible's batteries and they all sat listlessly on the floor in the cabin in the dark. No one spoke. No one had the energy to speak; nor did they want to waste their energy in another futile argument. Professor Spicer had dragged himself away from the control room, admitting defeat in his transmissions for help, without saying a word. He didn't need to; one look at his sullen face was enough to know the truth.

Eventually George shifted on the floor. 'How much... longer?' he asked breathlessly.

Peewee Peterson replied, almost gasping for air. 'Less than an hour, I think.'

'Not...how much... longer... do we have left... to live.' George forced out the words. 'How much... longer until my grandpa gets here.'

'Face it, son,' wheezed Marmaduke Spicer. 'I don't think he's coming.'

And with impeccable timing, George's mobile phone rang. He pulled it out of his pocket and clicked the green button.

'George?'

'Grandpa,' yelled George, finding breath from somewhere. 'Wait I'll put you on loud speaker. We're here.'

'How are things, lad?'

'Not good, Grandpa. We're running out of air fast. I hope you've got an answer.'

'Well, good news. I stole the porridge truck,' said Grandpa Jock.

'What?!' all six submarine survivors yelled at once.

'The porridge truck?' puzzled Allison. 'How's that good news?'

'That's great. That's just gosh-darn great!' The professor started off on another rant. 'We've pinned all our hopes on the madman in the skirt. Sorry, kilt!'

'Hullo? George? I can't hear you,' Grandpa Jock was saying. His voice was faint and tinny. 'There's a lot of noise at your end. I've swiped five big hoses from the fire truck too. And yon little beastie's here with me.'

The submarine fell silent. George ran to the glass as Chuck flipped the lights on. Muncher was nowhere to be seen.

'Is the commander with you?' asked Grandpa Jock. 'Tell him to get changed into his wet-suit!'

Chapter 27 - Truck

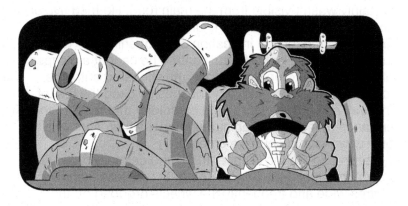

The first thing Grandpa Jock had done upon leaving the marquee was to find the keys for the massive, articulated dump truck that sat behind the tent filled with 22 tonnes of oatmeal. The driver had assumed nobody would have the nerve to steal such an obvious joyride that he'd left the keys under the sun-visor in the cab. It was the first place that Grandpa Jock checked.

The next thing he did was to sneak behind the fire truck and unscrew the five main hosepipes. Despite their great weight, he managed to stash them in the cab of the dumper, then jumped into the driver's seat and took off around the loch. Nobody saw him leave.

Except the film crew!

The journey around to the east bank of Loch Ness was a slow one and the road was long and windy. The dumper truck struggled to get up to 40mph on the straight, even with Grandpa Jock's foot heavily down on the accelerator. It was considerably slower around the bends so that the whole trip took almost an hour.

Even after that Grandpa Jock had difficulty in finding the hidden entrance to the cavern. It wasn't sign-posted and certainly wasn't visible from the main road. He tried five or six cut-offs down to the loch, jumping out of the cab each time to search for any indication of an opening. He was lucky that on his last off-road venture he caught a glimpse of the rocky outcrop that formed the sheltered entrance to the cavern. Trees and large bushes blocked the rest of the way and it was clear to the ex-soldier that most of the entrance must have been hidden under water. That was the only way the sub could've entered.

He ran back to the dumper truck and carefully reversed down onto the stony beach. The path was less than two metres wide and frequently the wheels dropped off the stones and into the loch. Luckily the water's edge was shallow and with a little skill and careful manoeuvring Grandpa Jock was able to bring the rear of the truck right into the small opening to the cavern. The massive wheels flattened a few bushes and exposed the entrance.

Grandpa Jock splashed down into the water then dragged the hoses from the passenger seat. These thick tubes were very heavy and the old man struggled to man-handle them round to the back of the dumper. He winced as he sat down at the edge of the water. Most of the air had already slipped out of his inflatable pants and he felt a sharp, shooting pain in his bottom as his piles objected to the cold stones.

With frantic fingers he coupled together the five hoses until he had one massive length of hosepipe. He stood up gingerly and connected the first pipe to the exit valve on the tanker. Then he ran around to the cab again and turned the engine on. That was the easy part of the rescue.

From the floor of the cab Grandpa Jock lifted a small plastic bag. Carefully he pulled out a grubby apron, walked around the truck and picked up the end of the conjoined hosepipes. Gingerly he stooped into the mouth of the cave and crawled through the short passageway. With his knees dragging on the gravel, he managed to hold onto the nozzle of the pipe and still keep the apron out of the water until the cave opened up inside. The water was teeming with the smaller plesiosaurs and towards the back of the cavern Grandpa Jock could see a herd of the larger beasts swimming majestically across the surface of the water.

He stood up and stretched, still holding the apron in his hand. He pressed his false teeth firmer into his gums and blew between his thumb and forefinger. A loud, sharp screeching whistle emanated from his lips and echoed around the cavern. Heads turned and dozens of pairs of eyes stared at Grandpa Jock.

He waved the white apron around his head. The creatures were initially attracted to this movement but soon lost interest and continued their graceful dance.

Grandpa Jock kept on waving and whistling for the next twenty minutes. He was on the brink of giving up when a small head popped up out of the water. Its nostrils twitched and its nose wrinkled. Slowly, curiously the little plesiosaur swam across towards the old Scotsman, who'd now bent down at the water's edge.

Grandpa Jock reached out and the plesiosaur allowed the old man to rub its forehead playfully. He held out the apron to the inquisitive creature, who sniffed again and let out a low moaning squeal.

'If I didn't know better, I'd say you sounded like Chewbacca from Star Wars,' chuckled Grandpa Jock and he threw back his head and growled like a wookie. The young plesiosaur tilted its head and just stared.

'OK, that was rubbish, but I need you to wait here for me.' And Grandpa Jock pulled out his mobile phone and speed dialled the number.

'George? How are things, lad?' He paused.

'Well, good news. I stole the porridge truck,' said Grandpa Jock, listening carefully.

'There's a lot of noise at your end. I've swiped five big hoses from the fire truck too. And yon little beastie's here with me.' Grandpa Jock stroked the nose of the baby plesiosaur. 'Is the commander with you? Tell him to get changed into his wet-suit!'

'Now take this. Find Allison!' he shouted and held out the nozzle of the hosepipe. 'Go on, find the wee girl, go on.'

Grandpa Jock threw his arms towards the tunnel and pointed. 'Take it, go on.' Again the little dinosaur looked at him bizarrely. 'Allison, find Allison,' he said and rubbed the apron over the animal's snout.

There was a split second of hesitation before a flick of its powerful tail propelled the plesiosaur up from the water and bit the hosepipe out of Grandpa Jock's hand. With a roll of its body, the marine mammal splashed backwards and disappeared below the surface.

Grandpa Jock began to dance out of the way of the coiled hose, which was unravelling itself and plunging down into the water, snaking after the dinosaur. It was unfurling fast and soon the first coupling had disappeared below the water. Then the second, as the hose continued to snake off in the direction of the Grand Canyon.

The third coupling eventually disappeared into the water too.

A few moments later the fourth joint slipped into the darkness. A horrible thought then struck Grandpa Jock. What if there wasn't enough hosepipe? What if it wasn't long enough? His master plan would be thwarted before he had a chance to flick the switch on the back of the dumper truck. The tube continued to reel out.

Suddenly the hose stopped. It just bobbed at the edge

74

of the water, whilst the remaining coils sat motionless on the stones. Grandpa Jock stared at the hosepipe. The coils were a metre in diameter; there were fourteen or fifteen coils of hose remaining. After that it was only the short tube attached to the dumper truck.

As quickly as the hose stopped the coils started to disappear into the water again. Grandpa Jock waited. If George was right, stage two wouldn't take as long. Commander Choppers should only take a few seconds to swim into the Grand Canyon. Grandpa Jock waited nervously.

The hosepipe came to a halt again. Then it yanked. Once, twice, three times, it danced in the water. Grandpa Jock didn't need telling again. He squeezed back through the small crevice to the outside world and pressed the big green button on the back of the dumper truck, marked 'elevate'.

The large green tank mounted to the dumper truck's frame rose up on the hydraulic arm until it was pointing down at a 60-degree angle to the ground. Gravity, with the help of the pneumatic pump would dispense the tank's contents through the hosepipes.

Grandpa Jock pulled down on the big lever and the pump began to churn. The hosepipe began to chug as the first of the 22 tonnes of oatmeal were flushed along towards the cavern's tunnel.

Grandpa Jock sat down carefully on the stones, the final bubble of air tooting out of his whoopee cushions. He smiled. This really was squeaky bum time.

Chapter 28 – Luck!

As soon as Grandpa Jock had said 'big hoses from the fire truck' everyone in the submarine knew what he was doing. The three young minds were just as fast, if not faster, than the greatest science geeks that America had to offer. This was Grandpa Jock they were talking about and his ingenuity knew no bounds. George, Allison and Kenny had known him long enough.

Commander Choppers had jumped into his wet suit as fast as he could whilst Peewee Peterson pushed and pulled the air tank out of the hatch. At the water's edge Peewee and the professor carried out all the checks necessary for a dive; the compression gauges, the mouthpiece and pipes as Choppers strapped the tank to his back.

He spat into his mask, rubbed the visor with a squeak and pulled the face piece over his head. He waited at the edge of the water, facing the tunnel towards the Grand Canyon.

George and Allison waited at the water on the other side of the submersible.

After what seemed like an eternity, a friendly little face popped up out of the water holding a nozzle in its jaws. Grandpa Jock's theory had been spot on – plesiosaurs like to play 'fetch!'

'That was lucky,' said George, more than a little relieved.

Grandpa Jock was sure he'd seen dolphins do the same kind of tricks on the TV and from the way the creatures had stared at him whilst he was in the submarine earlier he was sure these animals were just as intelligent as dolphins.

But there wasn't time for another game. Allison took the hosepipe from little Muncher's mouth and with George's help they ran round the sub and across the rocky ledge to where the scientists were waiting. Commander Chuck grabbed hold of the nozzle and dived into the water; the high intensity flashlight attached to his wetsuit bouncing beams under the surface.

Soon, Chuck was lost into the darkness.

George didn't think that the Grand Canyon was far from the ledge; the sub hadn't travelled for long once the cavern had started to drain. Choppers swam deeper into the hillside and he pulled the first coupling over the ledge behind him.

When he surfaced, Chuck was relieved to see he was back in the centre of the Grand Canyon with the plesiosaurs' toilet block on the right and the gaping chasm of a crack running down the cave wall to the left. He swam up onto the dinosaurs' dumping ground and climbed out onto the toilet ledge. This provided a solid platform to fire his porridge gun from and he let his mouthpiece slide off.

The acrid stench of stale urine caught the back of his throat and he choked loudly. There was a very fishy poo smell too and he almost lost the contents of his stomach for a moment.

But he was a marine and he had a job to do.

He held onto his lunch and yanked hard on the hosepipe three times and felt it vibrate in his hands. The oatmeal had a long way to travel so Chuck dug his feet in, stood firm and waited.

The trembling in the hose became stronger and stronger until the nozzle gave a sudden jolt and he knew he was armed and ready. This toilet ledge, with the dark passageway behind back down to England, was a little further away than Chuck would've liked but he knew he would have to use the arc of the spray to his advantage.

Aiming high, he pulled the handle towards him and an enormous sweep of oatmeal spewed out of the front of the hose, over the water and across to the fissure.

The oats splattered down into the water exactly in the middle of the jagged split, as Choppers held the hose tightly and continued to aim between the cracks of rock.

More and more oatmeal churned out and Chuck had to fight with the pressure in the nozzle to hold the arc steady. His arms were aching and his fingers throbbed as he squeezed the pipe into submission. Still the oats poured out relentlessly but by aiming his chest torch towards the cleft Chuck could see a bulging mass of porridge building up inside the gap.

The dry oats were swelling up and absorbing the water at the base of the crevice. This early oatmeal formed a stodgy foundation of porridge for the next wave of oat-flakes to rain down upon, creating another level of gluttonous barricade.

The pain in his forearms was almost unbearable but he fought on, taking strength from watching his wall of porridge build up inside the rift.

And as soon as the porridge had reached up over the water line, Chuck saw the loch begin to rise. The other tributaries and streams were still flowing into the Grand

Canyon but with the fault-line sealed up, the levels began to increase. Chuck hoped the ridge would soon begin to flood too, as the 22 tons of porridge oats was dumped into the deep water cavern.

By the time the last of the oatmeal shot from the hosepipe the porridge cement had filled the entire crevice. The water levels were now up to Choppers' waist and still rising. His work here was done. He checked the pressure gauge on his wrist to see that his tank was still twenty percent full, more than enough air to make the short trip back through to the central ledge.

He spat onto his mask again, slipped it on and dived into the loch. He used the hosepipe to pull his body through the water. His arms ached and his flipper feet did most of the propulsion. Eventually the beam of light from his torch caught a glimpse of the hull of the submersible, now fully submerged underwater again and he carefully manoeuvred himself around to the airlock. Chuck pulled the top hatch down and swivelled the locking wheel. Then he spun the second wheel and the water around him began to flush away.

Chuck picked up the hammer which was attached to a chain on the wall, banged against the airlock door and a loud metallic clang echoed around the sub. Suddenly he was pushed back against the wet wall, as the sub lifted off the ridge bed and became fully operational again. The professor must've been piloting the craft, keen to make their departure from their airless prison as the vehicle thrust forward.

Chapter 29 – Unidentified Unsinkable Underpants!

The trip back to the first cavern didn't take long and the submersible rose once again, much to the chagrin of the older plesiosaurs. Muncher was first to welcome them back and Chuck threw open the hatches to release and purify the stale air inside the submarine.

Grandpa Jock stood on the shoreline waving Allison's apron above his head and cheering as loudly as he could. His bum was still sore but he could live with that, knowing he'd done his part.

Professor Spicer appeared at the top hatch and shouted down.

'I believe we owe you a debt of gratitude, Mr Jock. Fine piece of thinking back there. Thank you, sir.'

'You're a genius, Grandpa!' shouted a small voice from inside the submarine as the craft sailed up to the shore and stopped just at the old man's feet.

'Come aboard, sir and we'll head back over to the harbour,' smiled Spicer, a little sheepishly and very much relieved. Grandpa Jock hopped up onto the sub with a helping hand from the professor and the two of them slid down into the ship's bowels. Once inside, the craft descended again.

'They'll be looking for their oat truck by now,' shrugged Grandpa Jock. 'Shame they can't go for their world record porridge attempt.'

'We'll leave the dumper truck hidden there, it's safe enough for now,' confirmed the professor. 'We'll need to organise a return trip to Grand Canyon though, to make the seal more permanent.'

And at that, the craft scraped and scratched through the narrow opening at the exit from the cavern. It certainly was a lot tighter since the latest land shift and Commander

Chuck thrust the throttle forward fiercely. With a squeal from the engines and a screech from the hull, the sub shot forward like a snot rocket and ploughed safely into Loch Ness.

'Looks like water levels have dropped in here,' said Peewee Peterson, checking his hydro-gauges. 'So England's lakes will be returning to normal again too.'

'I don't think we'll be swimming in Little Lake Pump for a wee while yet,' grimaced George, as the submarine drifted towards the surface of Loch Ness. Daylight shone into the cabin for the first time that day as the massive expanse of water spread out before them. The sky was blue, the mountains were a beautiful mixture of greens and purples and it felt good to be free once more.

'Let's enjoy the sunshine, folks,' suggested Professor Marmaduke, perhaps hoping to make amends for his short temper back in the cavern.

Commander Choppers stayed at the controls whilst the other six clambered up onto the top deck of the submarine. They drew in the fresh Highland air and basked with the warm sun on their faces. Yes, even in Scotland, thought George. The sub sailed on gently towards the harbour.

'You seem to be yourself again, professor,' smiled Allison.

'I don't like not being in control and I certainly don't like being wrong,' sighed Marmy. 'But I'm happy to say you kids have taught me a valuable lesson in trust today. Thank you.'

'I think I've learned a lesson on this holiday too,' admitted George, looking over at Allison, who blushed. Kenny stuck two fingers down his throat and made a coughing, yakking, barfing sound.

'Blergh! You two make me sick. Mr Jock, make them stop.'

And then, to the delight of everyone on deck Muncher appeared, splashing and diving in the water around them.

The cheeky little plesiosaur had obviously followed the sub from the main cavern.

'He wants to play 'fetch!' again,' laughed Grandpa Jock.

The professor, George, Allison and Kenny all joined in the hilarity and the small dinosaur seemed to enjoy the attention, showing off a little more by skimming across the water in front of the submarine.

'The wee rascal that he is,' chuckled Grandpa Jock. 'Dolphins play like that too. He just wants to entertain his audience.'

It was Peewee who snapped them back to reality.

'He'll have a bigger audience in a minute, sir. A worldwide one. Look!' Peewee was shouting and pointing over to a speeding motor boat.

'It's the police!' yelled Marmy. 'And they're coming this way!'

'And they're firing flares too,' screamed Allison. 'What are they doing that for?'

Two pops were heard from the police boat and a pair of rockets with trails of red smoke shot up into the air. Their boat bounced over the waves and sped towards the submarine.

'That's the Nessie signal,' shouted Marmaduke. 'Soon the loch will be crawling with boats. We have to get the little one out of here.'

'It's that blooming TV crew as well,' spat Grandpa Jock. 'They saw me leaving the marquee. I bet they're after me for stealing that porridge truck. It's all my fault!'

'Sorry Jock, you did the right thing but I don't care about your rescue right now, sir.' The professor had only one thought in mind. 'If they catch sight of our serpent on film, we might as well open the gates to a Nessie theme park right here.'

'Not if I can help it,' shouted Grandpa Jock and he

jumped onto the ladder and slid down into the submarine. Moments later, the old ginger Scotsman struggled back up onto deck carrying Commander Choppers' compressed air tank. He stepped to the back of the submersible, out of sight of the oncoming police boat. Grandpa Jock was breathing hard after the day's exertions and he was having doubts about the second part of his plan.

Marmy Spicer pointed to the little plesiosaur, who was swimming furiously back to the safety of the cave.

'He's not going to make it,' yelled the professor. 'It's too far and that speed boat will catch him up the rate they're gaining.'

'We need a diversion,' shouted George, not quite sure what he was hoping for. Grandpa Jock knew.

'Allison, close your eyes,' he ordered. 'George, are you ready to swim? Allison, close them!'

Allison didn't know why but she did as she was told. George nodded and slipped off his shoes.

Then Grandpa Jock slipped off his pants!

With one slick move, he reached under his kilt and whipped off his specially created haemorrhoid breeks. The whoopee cushions that were sewn into the buttocks were almost flat so they were easy to slip through the special pockets in the back of his knickers. Grandpa Jock's fingers moved swiftly as he carefully peeled the duct tape back from both bags.

He opened a cushion's mouthpiece with one hand and forced the air hose from the diver's tank into the first bag with the other. Grandpa Jock turned the valve and the little pink bag quickly began to fill with compressed air.

Once it was the size of an enormously over-inflated beach ball Grandpa Jock swopped bags, pinching the end of the first to stop the air escaping. The second whoopee cushion quickly blew up to the same size and he twisted the nozzles over the waistband of his big pants. Grandpa Jock finally sealed the cushions with their duct tape strapping again, looping it through the pockets.

'Quick, lad. Put this on!' shouted Grandpa Jock, knowing every second counted to save the secret of the Loch Ness Monster.

'What!' yelled George. 'You want me to wear your pants, Grandpa?'

'Yeah, like a jacket. C'mon, slip them over your shoulders, boy. It's an emergency.'

George didn't have time to think, as first one hand then the other slid through the leg holes of his grandpa's extra special pants. As his arms went in, George closed his eyes and tried not to think about any skids marks that might've been left on the gusset of the garment. The whoopee cushions were bobbing around his shoulders like a giant pair of Mickey Mouse ears.

Grandpa Jock's knickers were wrapped tightly around George's shoulders, high up on his chest. George felt as if he was wearing a bull fighter's bolero jacket (cool) ... made from y-fronted, big skid-marked pants (not cool).

'Sorry, lad,' Grandpa Jock said, holding his hands out. 'I wish it could've been me but I'm just getting too old.' And with that, he pushed George into the water.

'MAN OVERBOARD!' yelled Grandpa Jock.

'Man overboard!' 'Man Overboard!' 'Man Overboard!' yelled everybody else, quickly joining in.

The police motor boat spotted George in the water from a good distance away but didn't slow its speed. George bobbed up and down on the loch, trying to look as dinosaur-like as possible with his inflatable fart bags floating around behind him. The official craft was caught

in two minds, whether to rescue the stricken swimmer or continue to give chase to the unidentified floating object when they heard the panic-stricken shouts from the submarine.

They had no choice but to stop and join in the rescue of the young ginger haired boy and his giant inflatable underpants. George was pulled to safety rather harshly by the police and now they wanted answers.

'The lad just fell in, officers,' explained Grandpa Jock casually. 'Luckily we had these life-pants handy.'

'The camera crew over there claim to have footage of the Loch Ness Monster swimming near your craft,' stated the first officer.

'No, we never saw anything.'

'The Loch Ness Monster? Are you're kidding, really?'

'How did we miss that?'

'Have they been drinking, officer?'

'No sir, we didn't see anything like that, sir.'

'Are you calling me a liar?!' came the chorus of rejection and disapproval.

'Well, I think we should all look at the evidence on film,' said the second officer, inviting the submariners onto the police cruiser. 'Then maybe you'd like to amend your statements.'

Grandpa Jock gulped and led the way over onto the speed boat. Just as he stepped aboard, and whilst the officers were distracted helping Allison and the others cross between boats, Grandpa Jock snatched a glance over to the far side of the loch. He could just about make out the porridge truck hidden behind a thick clump of bushes and a dark, overhanging rock formation.

In the water, just for a second, he saw a ripple of pink and a delicate tail slip below the surface and disappear into the darkness. Grandpa Jock turned to see George watching too and he winked across. Muncher was safe.

The TV crew were too busy rewinding their digital film to see what was happening elsewhere. When everyone was finally on-board they flicked out the screen doors on their cameras and played their movie. George was impressed with the quality and clarity of the film; however, the footage was shot from quite a distance away and even when they zoomed in for a close-up the rocking and bouncing of the boat made it impossible to get an accurate shot of any creature.

A series of dark pink humps could be seen skimming across the surface of the water but never for more than a few seconds at a time.

'That's George's inflatable underpants,' said Grandpa Jock assuredly.

'Yes, sir. Biggest gosh-darned pair of fart pants I've ever set eyes on,' nodded Professor Spicer.

'Those aren't humps. That's George's whoopee cushions. Saved his life, so they did,' agreed Kenny.

'These gentlemen have been drinking, officer. Smell their clothes,' said Allison, sniffing the air.

'The young lady is correct, officer. I would say that was brandy.' Peewee took off his glasses to wipe them and sniffed the air again. 'Yup, brandy.'

'No, no, wait. We were covered in brandy at the porridge festival. There was an explosion,' protested the cameramen. 'We've not been drinking, officer. We've captured Nessie on film, honest.'

'Another likely story,' shrugged Grandpa Jock, now addressing the two policemen. 'Sorry officers, but as the only true Scotsman on board the boat, and as such, the most likely to profit from the massive surge in Nessie hunters, sightseers and tourists, I'm afraid I can't agree with these two unreliable eye-witnesses. All I see is a pair of extra big, blow-up breeks.'

The two police officers gave the matter some careful consideration but had no choice but to send them all back across to the submarine with a warning about over-crowding the deck and a reminder to carry the correct life-saving equipment on board. Underwear, no matter how inflatable should not be used as life preservers, they said.

As the police boat sped away, the cameramen were gobsmacked to watch their dreams of fame and fortune sailing off into the sunset.

Afterwards it was suggested that Grandpa Jock muttered 'Load of pants!' under his breath but this was never proven.

To this day the sighting of pink plesiosaur humps on Loch Ness was considered a hoax but officially classified as 'unidentified'.

Chapter 30 – Saboteur

Once back at the harbour the scientists dropped off George, Allison, Kenny and Grandpa Jock then set sail to retrieve the dumper truck from the mouth of the cavern. They didn't want to take any chances that the hidden entrance to the cave might be discovered.

Professor Spicer had already contacted a concrete company to order enough sand and cement to fill the fissure all over again. The porridge would do the job for now but something more permanent would be required.

However, the greatest minds in the scientific community were a little stumped as to what to do with the surplus porridge once it was replaced with the concrete. George had suggested feeding it to the plesiosaurs but Allison was appalled at that idea.

'You don't just go around feeding any old stuff to animals,' she complained. 'They have special diets.'

'But it's good porridge,' argued George with a smile.

'You could flush it down the toilet chute into England, if you wanted,' chuckled Grandpa Jock.

'That's not a bad plan, Mr Jock, sir,' nodded Marmaduke. 'Of course, it would eventually be eaten by small fish so there would be no harm to the environment. You may wish to check any rivers and lakes you visit in the next few months for traces of that record breaking breakfast cereal.'

The harbour was deserted. Without the oatmeal the Guinness Book of Records people had gone home disappointed, and the townsfolk of Drumnadrochit would have to wait until next year to break the record.

The four of them strolled along the street towards the fair ground. Way off in the distance, jumping the stone wall and clutching what looked like a golden, shimmering rolling pin was a small flame-haired boy.

Grandpa Jock nudged George, 'He looks like a wee burning match down there, doesn't he?'

'Grandpa! You're just jealous because his hair is redder than yours.'

'We won!' Hamish was shouting as he ran towards them. 'We won!'

It didn't take the excited lad long to cover the distance from the field to the group of four. All the time he ran he held aloft his prize, the Golden Spurtle of the World Porridge Championships. There was a purple and green ribbon tied around the handle and it glittered in the sunlight.

'We won, Mr Jock,' said Hamish, as he approached. 'We won... well, not you, really. You didn't win. Technically it's my name on the trophy but you deserve it.'

'How's my name not on the trophy?' Grandpa Jock looked a little crestfallen.

'Well, after you left I had to finish off the dish,' Hamish explained. 'But I got peckish and I ate all the raisins.'

'They were for the sauce!' yelled Grandpa Jock.

'I realise that now,' said Hamish. 'So I had to think of something else.'

'What did you do?' asked Allison suspiciously. After all, she was second in command of the Jock Squad.

'I borrowed some chocolate from the German team. They were using it for their Gateaux,' replied Hamish, a little guiltily.

'Borrowed? You mean you stole it!' accused Grandpa Jock. 'Well, I would never... ever steal... eh... I would... er... probably never steal... I mean I would...' The thought of the dumper truck popped in Grandpa Jock's head for a split second.

'I mean... I'd probably have done the same. Well done, young man.' Grandpa Jock shuffled nervously.

'You can't seriously advocate stealing, Mr Jock,' said Allison, forgetting about her ill-gotten rescue.

'It's okay,' said Hamish. 'I did offer to pay for it but they said 'nein, danke', whatever that means. Do you want to know what else I put in the sauce?'

'No, thanks,' said Allison sharply.

'Oh, I thought you'd like to know,' replied Hamish, a little sadly.

'No, Hamish.' Allison rolled her eyes. 'That's what 'nein, danke' means in German – no, thanks. And yes please, tell us what else you put into our recipe.'

Grandpa Jock leaned in. Hamish smiled broadly.

'I added the chocolate and.......' Hamish wiggled his eyebrows. 'One of my toffee bars!'

'Toffee bars?' yelled George, Kenny and Allison together.

'Yes, toffee bars,' echoed Grandpa Jock, beginning to drool. 'A chocolate toffee sauce. That's genius, lad!'

'But it was your porridge, Mr Jock,' beamed Hamish. 'And your heather-honey haggis too. But because I changed the recipe I couldn't enter it under your name. I'm sorry, Mr Jock.'

'Ach, no worries, lad,' said Grandpa Jock smiling and ruffling his bright red hair. 'I'm just glad the trophy came back to Scotland.'

As they stood there chatting Laird Baird staggered up to them, laden with cooking pots, pans and all sorts of utensils. There were even two big bunches of asparagus sticking out the top of a box.

'There you are, Jock,' he said, slightly out of breath and with his beard singed around the edges. 'They're packing the marquee away so I thought I'd take this stuff back to your tent.'

'How do you know where our tent is, sir?' asked George.

'Don't worry lad,' I heard all about your grandpa's tent building skills. I know exactly where it is.' Laird Baird grinned. 'Come on, give me a hand.'

They all began to help; picking pots and pans from Laird Baird's burden and soon the equipment and excess food was equally distributed amongst the six of them. As they strolled into their camp site Laird Baird said,

'Shame about the world record attempt though,' Laird Baird growled. 'I think that mad vicar must be behind the theft of our oats as well.'

'Er... yeah... sounds like it,' stammered Grandpa Jock, looking shifty and desperate to change the subject. 'But how about my young protégé, Hamish?'

'Aw Jock, he did a fine job, eh? Winning the trophy.'

'Aye, he did a grand job,' agreed Grandpa Jock, relieved the conversation was moving onto safer ground.

'And Allison,' added George. 'She did well on Sunday too.' Allison smiled across and Kenny rolled his eyes as if to say 'not again'.

'I'm proud of you too, lad,' said Grandpa Jock. 'You've learned your lesson and that's very magnanimous of you to say.'

93

'What does magnanimous mean?' asked Kenny, smiling. 'Stomach churning?'

'No, it means...' Grandpa Jock stopped. In the centre of the camp site was Grandpa Jock's tent and Allison's extension. Their tent was almost jumping.

'What the Heston Bloomingheck is that?' spat Grandpa Jock, dropping his pots and pans and running up to the canvas door. He pulled at the zipper and opened the flaps wide.

There, curled up in a knotted ball of rope and duct tape was Reverend McVicars. He'd been kicking at the sides of the tent for hours and looked relieved to see them.

'What are you doing here?' boomed Laird Baird.

'Clearly not sabotaging the porridge competition, that's for sure. Now, sorry reverend, but this might hurt a little.'

Grandpa Jock slipped his fingernail underneath the corner edge of the strip of duct tape covering Reverend McVicars mouth and yanked hard.

Rrrrrrrrrrrrrrrrrasp!

The tape came off with one sharp tug and a red rectangular weal began to appear around the vicar's mouth.

'Thank you so much. I've been here all night,' he winced. 'I kept kicking the tent but all the campers just gave me a wide berth, as if they were scared.'

'Well, er... I may have frightened a few of the neighbours when I was putting the tent up on Saturday,' admitted Grandpa Jock. 'But how did you get in here?'

'I was heading home after the poetry contest on Sunday when somebody sneaked up behind me and threw a bag over my head,' the vicar went on. 'Then they tied me up and threw me in here.'

'They?' asked Laird Baird raising one eyebrow.

'Oh yes,' replied the reverend. 'There were definitely two of them.'

'Shame you didn't get to see their faces though,' said Grandpa Jock, keen to find out who the real saboteurs were.

'No, but I'd recognise their smell.'

'Eh?'

Reverend McVicars went on, 'I've always thought Miss Mackinnon and Miss McParvis put far too much lavender perfume on. It really stinks, that stuff.'

'Mad Mackinnon and Pee Pants McParvis?!' yelled Hamish, his eyes gleaming with intrigue.

'Are you sure, vicar?' asked Laird Baird. 'They tried to set you up for this, you know.'

'I don't doubt it for a minute,' said the reverend, shaking his head. 'They never wanted the competition held on a Sunday in the first place. They said it was taking the good Lord's name in vain, on the Sabbath.'

'They tried to get me involved in banning the event but I don't mind. It's just a bit of fun and I'm sure God loves porridge as much as the next man.' Reverend McVicars smiled.

'So they came up with a plan to sabotage the entries.' Laird Baird thumped his fist into the palm of his hand. 'Even faking a fear of poetry to get closer to the porridge judging.'

'And they probably stole the oats and the dumper truck too,' shouted Grandpa Jock a little too eagerly.

George had a puzzled look on his face. 'If they did fix the dishes.... why did they eat their own rabbit poo?' thinking about the 'raisins' in Grandpa Jock's creation.

'Probably to make the whole thing look genuine,' gagged Laird Baird, remembering his own mucky mouthful. 'But they've disappeared now and gone on the run. Shouldn't be too difficult to capture them though, two old dears in tweed suits and sensible shoes.'

Chapter 31 – The Green Green Glass of Home

Laird Baird took care of the cold, hungry reverend, promising him a slap up feast at his ancestral home if he promised to remain quiet about the 'whole nasty business'. He'd just about managed to keep a lid on the sabotage affair, which was serious enough, but a kidnapping scandal could kill off next year's Porridge Championships.

'No harm done really,' Laird Baird kept repeating, hoping to convince himself, as much as the reverend.

They both wished Jock farewell and headed over to the little police station, to discreetly update the officers on the new culprits and recent developments.

Once they were gone Hamish and Allison got the fire started whilst Grandpa Jock started preparing another one of his specialities. George and Kenny were suspiciously quiet and were frequently seen holding clandestine conversations behind the tents.

Hamish joined them for dinner when he heard that Grandpa Jock was conjuring up a marvellous feast featuring haggis, turnips and potato. Hamish loved haggis almost as much as Grandpa Jock although George and Kenny insisted on taking their haggis with the left-over asparagus.

The two boys were even late for dinner too, boiling the stalks in a separate pan for five minutes before they joined Allison, Hamish and Grandpa Jock on the picnic blanket in front of the tents.

'I didn't know you liked asparagus, George,' asked Allison carefully.

'Love it,' replied George munching on another stalk.

'I didn't see you adding grass to that pot, did I, George?'

'No, no, you must be seeing things, Allison.'

'There's quite a pile there, lad,' nodded Grandpa Jock, pointing at the steaming plate of stalks, dripping in butter.

'We thought we'd use them up,' said Kenny, as innocently as possible, munching into the long, green shoots of vegetable. 'There were only about 50 or 60 of them.'

'And I'm impressed, Kenny. You haven't even tried to stick one up your nose,' laughed Allison. 'I think we might even trust you with the marshmallows next.'

The rest of the evening was spent in front of the campfire, talking pants and discussing the events of the last couple of days. They even managed to recite some more poetry. And Grandpa Jock thought the men from the Guinness Book of Records should've been told about the world's first pair of inflatable underpants but Allison convinced him that they didn't do an underwear section.

George even managed to think up a version of Reverend McVicars and his Dirty Holy Knickers but he promised not to mention it again after Grandpa Jock laughed so hard he spat his false teeth into the fire.

And Kenny did try to stick a melted marshmallow up his nose for old times' sake but the burnt crust broke and he dribbled gooey pink snot all the way down his t-shirt.

It was late into the evening when they said goodbye to Hamish but promised to visit again next year.

And by 10 o'clock the next morning, George, Allison, Kenny and Grandpa Jock were back on the train, southbound this time, on their way home. They were sharing a table of four and Grandpa Jock was perched awkwardly on one of the seats, reading the earlier edition of the local newspaper.

'Sitting comfortably, Grandpa,' sniggered George.

'No!' moaned Grandpa Jock. 'And you know fine well that I'm not. My over-inflated underpants were stretched beyond capacity and I'll have to buy another pair of whoopee cushions when we get home. My bum's killing me!'

'At least the lakes in England are filling back up with water again,' said Allison changing the subject. The headline on the front of the newspaper read 'Water Stroke of Luck – Lake Levels Leap!'

'Yes, and there's no mention of any wee beasties seen in Loch Ness yesterday,' smiled Grandpa Jock. 'Nor any unidentified, unsinkable underpants neither.' He winked across at George.

But George and Kenny were too busy whispering and giggling again.

'You go first.' 'No, you go,' 'I'll take the jar, you check first' 'Right!'

And with that Kenny jumped up and ran down the centre aisle of the train. At the end of the carriage, he opened the sliding door to the toilet and stepped in. The door slid shhhhhhhhhht behind him.

'He's bursting,' said George, as casually as possible.

Grandpa Jock raised one bushy eyebrow. 'I haven't seen you go to the loo this morning either, eh?'

'I'll go in a minute, Grandpa.'

Allison eyed George a little warily. He kept crossing his legs, fidgeting about on his seat and hiding something under his jumper. Allison suspected there was something going on but before she could start her enquiries Kenny was back from the toilet.

'Well?' asked George.

Kenny laughed. 'It's true, it really works.'

'No way!' gasped George. 'I'm checking mine.' And with that he sprinted off down the aisle.

Two minutes later he was back again, looking very smug.

'Well?' asked Kenny with a grin.

'Taa-daa!' And George thumped a glass jar down on the centre of the table. The jar was filled with a lime green, almost luminous liquid. Kenny laughed. Grandpa Jock and Allison sat back with disgusted grimaces on the faces.

'What's that?' they asked together, not sure if they wanted to hear the answer.

'It is true,' confirmed George proudly. 'Asparagus really does make your wee green.'

'Urgh, that's your wee?' squealed Allison.

'You pee'd in a pot?' choked Grandpa Jock, almost laughing.

'Yeah, and it really stinks too! Shall I take the lid off?'

'NO!' shrieked Allison.

'Get rid of it, George. Science is finished for the day,' said Grandpa Jock, trying to act a little more responsibly but secretly impressed with the boys' experiment.

When George returned from the toilet with an empty glass jar, Kenny was still laughing and Grandpa Jock was smiling. Allison was not amused.

'Reminds me of the Irish recipe at the porridge competition yesterday,' said Grandpa Jock with a wink. 'Pea green porridge, wasn't it?'

'My wee wasn't thick and lumpy, Grandpa.'

'No, but it was green, George,' said Allison, still screwing up her face as if she had a yucky taste in her mouth.

'And have I told you my favourite joke, boys?'

'What's that, Grandpa?'

'Well, you two have to say pea green soup after everything I say. Okay?'

'Got it,' replied Kenny. George just smiled. He'd heard this before.

Grandpa Jock started off. 'What did you have for your breakfast yesterday?'

'Pea green soup,' replied George and Kenny together.

'You too, Allison,' urged Grandpa Jock and Allison's lips began to crack into a smile.

'And what did you have for your lunch yesterday?'

'Pea green soup,' they all said in unison. They were all smiling now.

'And what did you have for your dinner last night?'
'Pea green soup,' came back the familiar reply. Grandpa Jock grinned widely.
'And what will you do when you go to the toilet?'
'Pee green soup!'

The End

The World Porridge Making Championship Recipes

The Entrants	Their Recipes
Espana (Spain)	*King Prawn Porridge Paella*
Le Petit Pompedous (France)	*Porridge de Tadpole dans le sauce béchamel*
The Germans	*Black Porridge Gateaux*
Heston Bloomingheck	*Snail Porridge*
The Jock Squad	*Heather-Honeyed Haggis Porridge with a Whisky-Caramel and Raisin Sauce*
Team Antarctic	*Penguin Porridge Pancakes*
Mexico	*Porridge Fusion – Crispy Porridge Nachos with Thistle Salsa and Turnip Guacamole*
Koreans	*Pak Choi Porridge with Five Spice Porridge Powder*
The Leprechauns - Ireland	*Pea Green Porridge*
Team India	*Mutton Dansak with a Whisky Infused Porridge*
Italia, Italia	*Porridge Pizza with Porridge Pesto*
Science Geeks - USA	*Popping Space Porridge!*
Al O'Ween (America)	*Pumpkin Porridge*
New Orleans Hill-Billies	*Porridge Gumbo*

Local Competitors

Old Mary McSpurtle	*Porridge Pancakes*
Wee Ned	*Deep Fried Porridge Bars*
Tony McAroni	*Porridge Pasta Parcels*
Jock Patel	*Garlic Porridge Pakora*
Angus Anstrutherer	*Pureed Porridge Pate*
Iona Weeboat	*Poached Porridge Pears with crème fraise*
Marcie Landels	*Pommel-horse Porridge*
Wee Hamish	*Heather-Honeyed Haggis Porridge with a Chocolate-Toffee Sauce*
Mexico – last year's winners	*Chilli Chocolate Porridge*

Author's Notes

Professor Marmaduke Spicer's name is an amalgamation from two key people involved in the history of the Loch Ness Monster.

George Spicer (and his wife) saw 'a most extraordinary form of animal' cross the road in front of their car on 22nd July 1933. This sighting was the first to spark off the modern day Nessie phenomenon.

Shortly afterwards, Marmaduke Wetherell, a big game hunter was publicly ridiculed in the Daily Mail, the newspaper that employed him. To get revenge, it is claimed that Marmaduke committed the hoax, now known as 'The Surgeon's Photo' with the help of a sculpture specialist, an insurance agent and a doctor who offered the exclusive pictures to the newspaper. This hoax story was exposed in 1999 but is disputed by Nessie enthusiasts, who ask why the perpetrators did not reveal their plot earlier to embarrass the newspaper.

Without them, the Loch Ness Monster may not have caught the world's imagination in the same way. 'The Surgeon's Photo' became the defining moment in Nessie legend.

The Gorgeous George Books

Gorgeous George and the Giant Geriatric Generator
The first Gorgeous George Adventure
Bogies, baddies, bagpipes and burps!
Farting, false teeth and fun!
Kindle: http://goo.gl/tXB7x4

Gorgeous George and the ZigZag Zit-faced Zombies

Sneezing, sniffing, snogging and snots. Zombies, zebras and zits!

Gorgeous George and the Unidentified
Unsinkable Underpants Part 1

Poo, plesiosaurs, porridge, pants! Monsters, mayhem & muck!

Gorgeous George and the Unidentified
Unsinkable Underpants Part 2

More monsters, more mayhem and more muck.
And pot-loads of porridge, poo, pumps and pants!

Gorgeous George and the Jumbo Jobby Juicer

Burgers, bottoms, baddies and burps.
Power pink, pumping and poop!

www.stuart-reid.com

Gorgeous George
...and the Giant Geriatric Generator

Bogies, baddies, bagpipes and bums!
Farting, false teeth and fun!

Gorgeous George and the Giant Geriatric Generator begins
when George witnesses something rather disturbing from his
bedroom window late one night.

People are disappearing fast and no one seems to care. Why are the
people of Little Pumpington so miserable? Why has his evil teacher
started smelling of wee? Why is Mr Watt so fat? Why does Mr Jolly
the Janitor collect hundreds of pairs of false teeth in a cupboard in his
workshop? And will Grandpa Jock fill his pants if he squeezes a wee pump
out too hard?

During detention George discovers a secret stash of soggy tea-bags
and a hundred boxes of broken biscuits hidden in a mysterious
tunnel beneath the school. Can his new friend Allison help,
even though she's just 'a boring girl'?

Can Gorgeous George (who's not really gorgeous at all) solve
these mysteries with the help of his Grandpa Jock, the wild-haired
ginger Scotsman, before he deafens the whole town
with his bagpipes?

Oh, and do not try the 'Burning Bag of Poo Prank' at home.

You have been warned!

Gorgeous George
...and the Zigzag Zit-faced Zombies

Sneezing, sniffing, snogging and snots! Zombies, zebras and zits!

A chemical experiment by the military has gone wrong and the toxins are now airborne. The pupils of Little Pumpington Primary School are breathing in the gas and their behaviour is becoming bonkers.

Do you still pick your nose? Do you sit next to someone in school who still picks their nose? Do they eat it, even in secret, underneath their hand when they think no one else is watching? The Little Pumpington nose-pickers are taking over the school and their own bogies are not enough any more; they need to eat everybody else's too.

These psychotic snot-zombies are on the rampage, feasting on the nostril contents of the entire town and the army will do nothing to prevent them.

Can Gorgeous George, Allison and Crayon Kenny find a cure before the military decide to blow up the school? With the help of Grandpa Jock, Ben and Barbara and a box full of the tissues, they must stop the snot-zombies biting their booger-crusted fingernails to the bone.

Parents will not be able to read this book. This book is for strong-stomached children only, so no wimps need apply. This is the last taboo known to mankind and way beyond the comprehension of adults. The older you are, the yuckier this book will be. You have been warned!

Must... have... bogiieeeeeeeeeeeeeeeeees!

Gorgeous George
...and the Jumbo Jobby Juicer

Burgers, bottoms, baddies and burps. Power pink, pumping and poop!

Right, before we start let's get one thing straight; a jobby is another word for a poo... nothing more, nothing less. It's not rude, it's not swearing, it's just a little bit cheeky. And it's very Scottish!

The circus is coming to town and Grandpa Jock has almost wet himself with excitement. George's suspicions are aroused when the circus elephants begin dumping piles of pink poo on the pavement.

And the circus chimps are poop scooping the pink stuff into pails and taking it home. Is the delightful dung really just good for the garden or is there something more sinister going on?

Why are all of the country's elephants moving to a secret animal sanctuary? Why are the fields around Little Pumpington growing nothing but beetroot? Why are the burgers from McDoballs fast food restaurant so darn tasty? And what will happen to Crayon Kenny's little brother now that he has stuck five plastic soldiers up his bum? (Don't try this at home!)

Grandpa Jock sniffs a mystery, George sniffs the elephants' fear and Crayon Kenny sniffs his little toy soldiers. Is Allison the only sane person in the town? Even she is becoming addicted to the latest range of delicious cheeseburgers, chips and the new energy drink, Power Pink.

More poo, pee and pumps with Gorgeous George, so strong stomachs need only apply.

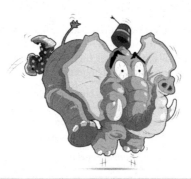

For Gorgeous George T-Shirts, Cups, Bags, Notepads, Phone/iPad Cases and MANY other products, please visit

http://www.redbubble.com/people/coldbludd/

collections/405936-gorgeous-george

THANK YOU!

About the author, Stuart Reid

Stuart Reid is 48 years old, going on 10.

Throughout his early life he was dedicated to being immature, having fun and getting into trouble. After scoring a goal in the playground Stuart was known to celebrate by kissing lollypop ladies.

He is allergic to ties; blaming them for stifling the blood flow to his imagination throughout his twenties and thirties. After turning up at the wrong college, Stuart was forced to spend the next 25 years being boring, professional and corporate. His fun-loving attitude was further suppressed by the weight of career responsibility, as a business manager in the retail and hospitality industries in the UK and Dubai.

Stuart is one of the busiest authors in Britain, performing daily at schools, libraries, book stores and festivals with his book event Reading Rocks! He has appeared at over 950 schools and has performed to over 200,000 children. In 2015 Stuart was invited to tour overseas, with visits to schools in Ireland, Dubai and Abu Dhabi, performing for 120 princes at the Royal Rashid School For Boys.

He has performed his energetic and exciting book readings at the Edinburgh Fringe Festival, has been featured on national television, radio and countless newspapers and magazines. He won the Forward National Literature Silver Seal in 2012 for his debut novel, Gorgeous George and the Giant Geriatric Generator and was recently presented with the Enterprise in Education Champion Award by Falkirk Council.

Stuart has been married for over twenty years. He has two children, a superman outfit and a spiky haircut.

About the illustrator, John Pender

John is 37 and currently lives in Grangemouth with his wife Angela and their young son, Lucas, aged 6.

Working from his offices in Glasgow, John has been a professional graphic designer and illustrator since he was 18 years old, contracted to create illustrations, artwork and digital logos for businesses around the world, along with a host of individual commissions of varying degrees.

Being a comic book lover since the age of 4, illustration is his true passion, doodling everything from the likes of Transformers, to Danger Mouse to Spider-man and Batman in pursuit of honing his skills over the years.

As well as cartoon and comic book art, John is also an accomplished digital artist, specialising in a more realistic form of art for this medium, and draws his inspiration from acclaimed names such as Charlie Adlard, famous for The Walking Dead graphic novels, Glenn Fabry from the Preacher series, as well as the renowned Dan Luvisi, Leinil Yu, Steve McNiven and Gary Frank.

John has been married to Angela for 7 years and he describes his wife as his 'source of inspiration, positivity and motivation for life.' John enjoys the relaxation and stress-relief that family life can bring.

Photography is another of John's pleasures, and has established a loyal and enthusiastic following on Instagram.

WR TING**RULES**OK

Writing Rules OK is Stuart Reid's creative writing workshop dedicated to inspiring children, young people (and teachers) to become aware of their unique power as writers, narrators and creative thinkers!

Each of the five modules looks at the specific elements of creative writing and includes exercises, classroom tools and homework sheets. The modules cover Genre, Plotting, Characters, Openers and Descriptives and these workshops can be classroom based, in small groups or as one-to-one coaching.

Writing Rules OK provides children and young adults with a basic knowledge and understanding of creative writing, with an opportunity to develop their own storytelling talents. There are several exercises included with each module, based on levels of ability, and includes Fast Finisher Extension Tasks, so whether your children are complete beginners or already becoming budding authors there's an exercise or two in each module to stretch everyone.

And there's no limit to the number of pupils or classes that can use the sessions; once you've bought each module, you can use them as often as you like. Although generally aimed at pupils between the ages of 8 and 14 years, each module lasts approx 1 hour, consisting of approx 15 minutes of audio summary and positioning, along with text-based exercises and worksheets.

www.writingrulesok.com

Lightning Source UK Ltd.
Milton Keynes UK
UKOW06f0120051117
312148UK00004B/196/P